The Texas Pistol

The Texas Pistol

WILL COOK

Sagebrush
Large Print Westerns

Library of Congress Cataloging-in-Publication Data

Cook, Will.
  The Texas pistol / Will Cook
    p. cm.
  ISBN 1-57490-269-5 (alk. paper)
  1. Big Bend Region (Tex.)—Fiction. 2. Large type books. I. Title.
  PS3553.O5547 T45 2000
  813'.54—dc21   00-024538

Cataloguing in Publication Data is available from the British Library and the National Library of Australia.

Sagebrush Large Print Westerns are published in the United States and Canada by Thomas T. Beeler, Publisher, PO Box 659, Hampton Falls, New Hampshire 03844-0659. ISBN 1-57490-269-5

Published in the United Kingdom, Eire, and the Republic of South Africa by Isis Publishing Ltd., 7 Centremead, Osney Mead, Oxford OX2 0ES England. ISBN 0-7531-6253-9

Published in Australia and New Zealand by Bolinda Publishing Pty. Ltd., 17 Mohr Street, Tullamarine, 3043, Victoria, Australia. ISBN 1-74030-009-2

Manufactured by Sheridan Books in Chelsea, Michigan.

To Carl and Lois Kromer—who listen often to the voice of the wind.

The Texas Pistol

CHAPTER ONE

TWICE DURING THE EARLY MORNING HE CUT BACK ON his trail and saw nothing, but the third time he did this, he paused near a rise of ground and saw the Comanche working his way slowly across a swale less than two miles behind.

Judging from the way the Comanche tracked Brazos Caine surmised that he was young and not too experienced, for he moved too slowly and made too many mistakes.

The land was massive and mountainous around this crooked valley and the hillsides were dark with cedar and scrub pine. Brazos had been moving along the valley's edge where the hills were smaller and somewhat rounded. He followed natural breaks in the land, staying to the higher ground where he commanded a clear view. But now he led his pack horse into the gullies and denser vegetation.

Brazos was a young man, no more than twenty-two or three but by 1840 Texas standards a wealthy one, for his armament was the latest and finest obtainable. He wore the fringed buckskins of a mountain man. His leggings were the buffalo-hide wrap-arounds of the Comanche, but the tops were wolf hide with the leather foxtails of the Kiowas. Around his waist was cinched a wide leather belt and on it hung his bowie knife, two .38 caliber Colt's Texas pistols with nine-inch barrels, a short battle hatchet, plus the powderflask, shot pouch, cap box and extra cylinders to serve his pistols.

On his face was a naked awareness, an instinctive alertness born of continual danger. His eyes were dark, his hair taffy-colored and worn shoulder length. He had come far and had been away long; his clothes were many-windowed and his pack horse showed ribs like the fingers of a fist.

Picketing the horse high in screening brush, Brazos Caine released the rawhide ropes binding the load of furs and lowered them to the ground. Then he turned and began to run along the trail he had just traveled. He moved with surprising speed and almost no sound, the soft soles of his moccasins touching the ground lightly.

Selecting a creek he had crossed an hour before, Brazos waded along the winding length until he found a spot no wider than the spread of his arms. Glancing along the bank, he found a stand of stout willows and moved into them, careful not to leave the slightest impress that would betray him.

Slipping his twelve-inch knife from his belt, he began to work. He notched a heavy stick and balanced it between two stones for a trigger. Cutting a longer stick, he laid it in the stream across the trail, hooking the blunt end into a bent sapling. When touched, the trigger would be released. Dead brush was piled around the bent sapling, and on one end Brazos' knife was fastened into a split. Breaking long buckskin thongs from his sleeves, he tied the knife securely so that it was pointed down-trail.

With his trap set, Brazos worked his way upstream to the thicket that hid his horse.

He had traveled perhaps a quarter of a mile when he heard a sharp scream, then he smiled faintly to himself and went on. His Comanche had found the knife.

Retrieving his pack horse, Brazos Caine cut once again west and by sundown was fording the Rio Grande. Once again he was in the Republic of Texas.

There was not much in the Big Bend country save the towering mountains and vast desert reaches, yet never did he return across the Rio Bravo but what he paused on this high promontory to look at this land.

A few white men lived here in scattered settlements, but the population was mostly Comanche and Coyotero Apache who called no man, red or white, friend. This was a primeval land where the hunter could become the hunted in the space of an hour. Texans fought Indians and Mexicans, and they in turn made war upon each other.

Leaving the high break of land, Brazos Caine slanted his course to the northwest and, by full darkness, raised the lights of Ryker's settlement. Ryker had built his settlement against the sheltering breast of a timber-covered hillside. Directly behind the main building was a cliff, the bare walls rising nearly a hundred feet from the valley floor. In the immensity of this land, the settlement was a mere scratch; four buildings fronting a ribbon of dust that would soon be ankle deep mud with the coming rains.

The largest of Ryker's four buildings was the store, a square, two-story structure built like a fort with battlements at each of the four corners. The other three were little more than three-sided sheds with sod roofs.

The nearest settlement to Ryker's was Fort Davis, two hundred miles to the north, but to the three dozen people living here it did not matter; they would never think of traveling so great a distance. This was their fifth year here; their fifth year of scratching a bare living from this hostile soil; the fifth year of poverty and death without relief, and without complaint.

Through the fleshed bullhide windows of Ryker's a feeble candlelight dribbled. Brazos walked down the strip of dirt road to unload his horse and stable it in one of the sheds. His bundle of pelts weighed nearly a hundred and eighty pounds, but he shouldered it with little effort and entered Ryker's store.

Inside, the store was sectioned into four quarters, the one on the right housing the trade goods freighted in twice yearly from Fort Davis. The barroom was directly across from this, connected by an archway, while in the back Ryker kept living quarters for himself and his two daughters. The upstairs had a wide gallery running around the walls, and four sleeping rooms were available in the back, an accommodation to anyone foolhardy enough to venture into this troubled land.

The bins and shelves along the walls were split cedar, shaved with an ax to some semblance of smoothness. The stairs were half-logs, bucked to six-foot lengths and notched for a staircase. Heavy tall candles reposed in wall brackets with tin mirrors backing them for the diffusion of the feeble light.

The women congregated in the store section and the low run of their talk was audible when Brazos Caine stepped into the doorway. The men were together in the barroom, gathered around a keg of blue ruin. The bar itself was a huge log buried in the dirt floor, its top smoothed with an ax.

Heads turned as Brazos Caine threw down his pelts and stepped up to the bar. "I've walked a spell and my thirst's a whoppin' big one. Put a dram in th' cup of these gents, while you're at it, Ryker."

Ryker poured and tin cups clanked, then everyone relaxed and waited for Brazos to speak. But the silence of the hills and far lands was still upon him and he lapsed into silence that sawed at their nerves.

Jubal Caine, Brazos' father, stood at the far end of the

4

bar, a huge man, heavily whiskered. Like his son, he wore a combination of Indian trappings and white dress. His calfskin coat was worn hair-side out and his pants were buckskin, the bottoms tucked into his wrap-arounds. On his belt was a Green River knife with a ten-inch blade, a buffalo-horn powder flask, and a short-barreled Texas pistol.

"Good trip?" he asked, his voice a rumble in the silence.

"Middlin'," Brazos said and drained his whiskey. "The Comanches are gettin' pesky. Man can't hardly trap without gettin' an arrow through him."

"Figured you might have been with Martin," Jubal said. "He come back a day or two ago, got roarin' drunk, then went out to his place."

"Those are fine pelts you fetched," Jeb McClintock said. He leaned against the bar, drawing on a clay pipe. McClintock was slat-lean, white-haired, and his face was clean-shaven except for the side whiskers and drooping mustaches. His clothes were store-bought and indicated hard service; the coat was beginning to get threadbare at the cuffs and elbows and large patches covered the knees of his pants.

"Must be two hundred dollars' worth of plews there," McClintock went on. "That's good money for three months' work."

"You could say that," Brazos admitted. "There's plenty more, Jeb. You just got to go get 'em."

McClintock pondered Caine's words as though wringing a rag dry, squeezing it until there was nothing left. Finally he said, "A man's place is here in the settlement, not roamin' all over God's creation for worldly goods." McClintock's pipe gurgled when he drew on it. "I'm closin' the settlement to further travel

5

until the trouble with Emiliano Esqueda is over. That's what this here meetin's about."

Brazos Caine straightened and looked at Jeb McClintock. "I wouldn't let the President's commission go to your head now, was I you. I come and go as I please. Just remember that."

"No use to bicker," Jess Olroyd grumbled. He was standing near Brazos' father, tall, lanky, with long whiskers tucked into the collar of his homespun shirt. Olroyd's three sons squatted along the wall with McClintock's four. "I'm tired of trouble," he went on. "Time's come to whup that Mexican proper so's a man can work the land in peace." He gave McClintock a blunt stare. "You've been sayin' you was goin' to catch that varmint until my ears is plumb wore out listenin' to it."

McClintock's head came around quickly and his eyes were filled with a sudden intolerance. "I had words with Martin over his tone the other night. It appears to me that you've a mind to walk in his steps."

"I didn't say that," Olroyd hastened to amend. "I don't cotton to Martin any more'n you do, but it's high time a man ought to be able to raise a crop without gettin' it burned or gettin' shot at while he gathers it."

There were nine other men in the room, quiet men who listened better than they talked. They were clad in rough homespuns and each man had his cap-lock rifle by his side; the powder horns hung on rawhide thongs across their bodies.

One of them, a blocky man with a swarthy face and deceptively mild eyes said, "Was we half Injun like some, we'd be able to afford a repeatin' pistol."

Brazos turned half around and looked at Bushrod Povy. "Was you less lazy, you wouldn't be livin' in a

6

hole in the ground and eatin' out of one dish. You're too tired to plow and fishin' too slow. Your woman goes ragged and your young ones are half-starved. Where th' hell's your pride, man?"

The words fell like blunt strokes of an ax and a tense silence followed. Povy's lips worked jerkily, then he stepped away from the bar, took off his powder horn and drew his knife. "I'll cut you up for that," he said softly and took a forward step.

McClintock moved between them and stood rockstill. "Hold!" he commanded. "As an officer of the Republic of Texas, I command you to drop this now! We'll get nowhere quarrelin' among ourselves." He glanced at Brazos. "Was I you, I'd spend more time on the land and less in the hills with that savage, Martin." He addressed all of them. "The nearest militia is at Fort Davis and we can't call on them. It is my responsibility to organize a troop here and, mark me, I intend to do it. Trade and roads we can do without, but Emiliano Esqueda is something that must be taken care of now. I intend to catch that man and hang him!"

"You figure on crossin' the Rio Bravo after him?" Brazos asked.

Jess Olroyd and the others waited patiently. There was no more talking from the store section and Brazos knew the women were listening. McClintock scowled, trying to probe beneath Brazos' easy manner for the hidden meaning. Finally he said, "I've half a mind to do just that."

"You know where he is?"

"At the moment, I don't," McClintock admitted, "but with a well-armed company behind me, I could soon find out."

"You'll never find his place," Brazos said flatly.

7

"This personal quarrel between you and Esqueda is pullin' us into somethin' we don't like, I'd say."

"Speak for yourself," Anse Moreclay said. He stood against the wall with his two sons, a raw-boned man with slight tolerance for any idea not his own. He lived on the flats with the others, his sod cabin a monument to a lifelong accumulation of careless habits. "I like Jeb McClintock's way better'n yours, Caine. I say let's kill 'em all, every mother and son. Maybe you and that animal, Martin, can make friends with the Injuns, but damned if I'm goin' to."

"Hold on a spell," Brazos cautioned. "Just because I go into the Comanche and Apache country don't mean I'm friendly with 'em."

"That's your story," Moreclay said. "No man can tell me another man can live three months among 'em and not get caught. You take me for a fool?"

"Some time ago," Brazos said and smiled faintly. He had a smooth face, unlined by trouble or the worries that plagued these men. His eyes crinkled with some inner amusement and he waited with calm patience while Moreclay digested the insult.

McClintock slapped the bar with the flat of his hands. "I've heard enough of this. We'll organize our company tonight and leave in the morning."

"I'm against any hasty moves now," Olroyd said.

"I'm in command," McClintock said, brushing Olroyd's comment aside, "and I've come to a decision. Since both Brazos and Martin are back, we'll use them to scout. Countin' Povy and Moreclay and Sykes, that'll make sixteen men, a goodly force, I'd say."

Jubal Caine frowned. "Seems to me that some of these lads are a little young for horse marines. Your own Roan and Antrim is only twelve and fourteen, or

8

thereabouts. Sykes' younguns ain't much older."

"I've considered that," McClintock said, "and in battle they will suffice."

"Well, goddamned if mine will!" Olroyd snapped. "Ray's twenty come green-up and what he does is his own business, but Jethro and Clem is too blamed young. I reckon they'd hold their own in a cut-and-claw fight, but I don't want anythin' to happen to 'em." He paused to rub his palms together. "Them younguns is all I'll get with the ol' woman makin' me sleep alone."

"My thoughts *were* for the women," McClintock stated. "Left here alone, the young ones wouldn't be worth a hoot in case of attack. But in the field, under my command, it will be a different story. The store here is sound and can be defended. I suggest that the women stay right here while we are out."

There was a moment's muttering among the men, then the majority of them nodded in agreement. Brazos made no comment until this had died down, then told McClintock, "Martin and me ain't goin', Jeb. We aim to start for Fort Davis with our plews."

"To increase your worldly riches?" McClintock's eyes blazed. "For shame!"

"That's what we're all workin' for, ain't it? To get ahead?" Brazos shook his head. "Jeb, I don't mean to quarrel with you, but I don't want to fight Esqueda. Had you left him alone in th' first place he wouldn't be hatin' us right now."

"I see," McClintock said flatly. "Caine, I know you have tried to undermine my position here in the settlement right along. If you carry it further, I will have to take steps to have you tried for treason to the Republic of Texas!"

"Mighty strong talk," Jubal Caine said softly.

Several other men murmured their agreement. Obviously a serious split was in the making. McClintock felt this but was helpless to mend the rent in their strength. He was firmly convinced that he was right and that Brazos Caine was wrong. The Texans were the conquering people and the Mexicans had to give way to them—give way or be defeated by force of arms.

"You won't try me," Brazos said mildly. "You won't be around to do it if you find Esqueda. He'll wipe you out to a man."

"I have never feared an idle boast or a threat," McClintock said pompously. "Caine, I see through your scheme—grow rich while the others fight for the land, then crowd me from my position as leader by the power of your gold. I warn you now, Caine; on that day one of us will die, for my authority comes from the President of the Republic of Texas."

Brazos stared at the old man, then shook his head and turned away, his elbows hooking the edge of the log bar.

"We leave in the morning," McClintock said flatly, and for Brazos Caine's benefit, added, "all of us."

The meeting broke up then and Brazos went into the store where the women waited. The room was long and smelled strongly of green coffee and spices. From a bin of dried apples, Brazos took a handful and munched on them. Several of the other men came into the store and went to their women, but the majority stayed by the bar until the jug of blue ruin was empty.

Jeb McClintock's daughter, Emma, was in the far corner and Brazos sauntered over. "I seen Martin," he said, out the side of his mouth.

"Why didn't you tell the others?" Emma asked. She was a young girl but woman-figured.

10

"They get het up too easy," Brazos said. "He wants to see you again. Tonight, if you can get out for a spell."

"I don't know," she said, shooting a glance at her mother. "She thinks you'n me are keepin' company."

"Let her think it," Brazos said. "You goin' to meet him or ain't you? I got to give him the signal if you are."

"She watches me close," Emma said. She raised her eyes and looked at Brazos. "Why does Papa hate Martin?"

"I don't know," Brazos said, deliberately evading the question. "I guess he's too independent and don't knuckle down to your pa. Your ma's scared some of it'll rub off on you if he hangs around. One of these days you'll be takin' up with a man proper like and she don't want it to be Martin."

"He's nice to me," Emma said wistfully. "You better go. Mama's lookin' at you."

Brazos edged away from the girl, moving toward the front door. Zelia McClintock blocked the way with her angular body. "Emma's been raised for a proper girl, Brazos Caine. If your intentions ain't honorable, I'll have Jeb take a whip to you!"

"Why, I—" He floundered, then went outside and leaned against the rough logs. A voice from the darker shadows startled him.

"You're going too far with the McClintocks. Let Martin take his own chances."

Swiveling his head quickly, Brazos leaned forward and saw Martha Olroyd standing against the wall six feet from him. He felt a sharp pull, a quickening within him, as though he had just completed a successful stalk on an elk. There was nothing shy about this girl; there was a restrained boldness in her eyes and the set of her

11

full lips. Lips fashioned for pleasing a man, he decided.

"The McClintocks don't scare me," he said, his voice cool and detached from his thoughts. "McClintock's a fool. He's got the settlement buff'loed."

"But not you, is that it?"

"I make up my own mind, same as Martin does," Brazos said flatly. "Emiliano Esqueda wanted to get along with us, but Jeb McClintock fixed things so's he couldn't. I just don't blame Esqueda for everything, that's all."

"Are you really going to Fort Davis in the morning?" Martha asked softly.

"Sure," Brazos said. "McClintock ain't going to get Esqueda. He'll wear out his horses and maybe get someone killed; I don't want no part of it."

"Maybe he's right, Brazos. Maybe you ought to think of the others and not yourself."

He grunted and fell silent for a moment. "Not me. I come here just as hog-poor as anyone else did. I built my cabin and laid away my stores and I'm beholden to no man. I cheated nobody and nobody can say I did."

"There's no arguin' with you, is there?"

"I reckon not," he said and turned his head as Martha's mother came to the doorway. She saw them together and her face mirrored a momentary displeasure.

She said, "Come in out of the chill, girl," and turned back inside.

Martha glanced at Brazos and said, "Think hard on it."

He nodded and watched her go into the building and after she passed from sight, walked toward one of the three-sided sheds and spread his buffalo robe for the night.

Out on the flats a coyote cried and Brazos listened. A moment later the sound came again and Brazos answered. He settled back on his robe and watched the front door of Ryker's. Emma McClintock came out and disappeared immediately.

Martin, Brazos decided, was like an animal, shy of human company. Yet Martin could not live without it. He lay back and listened to the night sounds, feeling an odd sense of shame for having arranged these many meetings between Martin and Emma McClintock.

People, he thought, ought to show themselves in the daylight. Not sneak around in the dark.

CHAPTER TWO

IF THERE WAS A FLAW IN THE BARTER SYSTEM OF trade, it lay in the fact that the profits were lopsided, with the producer coming out with the least. Since Ryker was the trader and took grain and jerked beef and hides for staples, then ran the risk of transporting these items through seven hundred miles of hostile country, the profit on almost all transactions in the settlement ended in his pocket.

Jeb McClintock did not like this, and it afforded him a topic of conversation whenever he could find a sympathetic listener. In the morning, while the women fixed the meal, he gathered the men around him and began a long lecture on profiteering.

Since the establishment of the settlement in this valley, the general policy had been to pay a 5 per cent tithing in grain, hides or beef, to be kept at Ryker's store in case of bad crops, marauding Indians or acts of God. From these stores the women drew the corn meal and jerked beef that made up this morning's breakfast.

Jeb McClintock stopped his harangue long enough to

13

eat. The table was the bar, the food was dumped in piles along the outer edge and men ate with their knives, scraping the wood clean when finished. The men held their beards out of the food while they lifted their broad blades.

Brazos went outside when he finished and stopped his new bowie knife against an ash ax handle. In Ryker's kitchen he heated water for his shave. Most frontiersmen chopped their beards off square by grabbing a handful of hair and whacking at it with a knife. Some, like Jess Olroyd, let it grow until it touched their belly; but Brazos preferred a smooth face.

After his shave he went outside in the weak sunlight and stood against the wall. Jeb McClintock had the men gathered around him and was saying, "It is not my plan to cross the river after Esqueda. I choose to ambush him on this side when he crosses to meet his Comanche and Apache friends."

"Not Apache," Brazos said mildly. "They cotton to no man."

"That's a heap of river to cover," Jess Olroyd said. "Can't say as I know the country too well."

"Brazos Caine does," McClintock stated. "Which brings to my mind that there's a likely crossing this side of the Mission Boquillas. Fair-sized bluffs overlookin' the river. We could catch him in midstream."

"There's nothin' sayin' he's got to cross there," Brazos said. "There's two other places he could use. The one farther down and the one near San Carlos mission." From inside his shirt he withdrew a twist of tobacco and bit off a chew. He watched the expression on the faces and saw everything from open hunger to stiff-necked pride that denied hunger existed.

That was the way things were here. It got so bad a

14

man could feel guilty because he owned a little tobacco and a full powder flask. Brazos put the tobacco away and said, "I'll go along with you as far as Martin's place, then you can forage for yourself. Ryker's stock is gettin' pretty low and Martin and I thought we'd try to get a string of carts through to San Felipe de Austin."

McClintock frowned and blew on his mustaches.

"We were talkin' about Esqueda," he said. "We'll discuss whether you go or don't go later." He swept the gathering with his eyes. "The way I see it, we're shaky. Last year was a poor one for crops, with the raidin' and all. This year won't be much better. Was Esqueda to make one strong swoop through here we wouldn't have a settlement. We need food supplies and tools so's a man can work. I see no other way but to get Esqueda first, then think about gettin' wagons through."

"Give me the sixteen men," Brazos offered, "and I'll take you all the way to New Orleans."

"That makes sense," Olroyd said quickly. "By grab, I'd like to see that town again."

"No," McClintock said flatly. "We'll go ahead with my plan. I've told Ryker what we'll need and my boys will load it." He turned to his oldest son. "Asa, bring up the animals. See that they're packed. We'll leave within the hour."

The older men stood round while the young men gathered the horses and carried supplies from Ryker's store. Ryker came out, a short man with a bald head and a mouth crowded with gold teeth. He stood aside and watched, then sidled over to where Brazos waited.

"You and Martin going to try to get through?"

"Wouldn't be surprised," Brazos said softly. "Old Iron Pants thinks otherwise."

"Th' damned fool's got the cart before the horse,"

15

Ryker said in a testy voice. "You could get a column through with an armed guard, couldn't you?"

"Martin and me went to New Orleans last year," Brazos said. "Made two trips to Fort Davis. I reckon we could get wagons through."

Ryker grunted and fell silent, his thick lips pursed. "You been thinkin' about my plan?"

"Some. I don't want it."

"Why not?"

"Just don't," Brazos said. "I got my trappin' to do; things of my own to keep me busy. Besides, McClintock has the President's commission. How do you get around that?"

"It can be done," Ryker said softly. "Brazos, he's done fine up to now, but he's no good any more." He looked at Jeb McClintock, who walked around the animals, inspecting the lashings, issuing countless orders. "Damn old turkey! I got a grain shed full and can't get it out. Can't he forget that damn Mexican long enough to see what's goin' on?"

"Ask him. He'll tell you about his new plan." Brazos spat tobacco juice in the dust.

"See? You don't like it and neither do some of the others. You sure you ain't goin' to change your mind?"

"I'm sure," Brazos said. "Martin and me's goin' to San Felipe de Austin with our plews. Might be able to bring you back two carts of stuff."

"Be no use," Ryker said. "I couldn't pay for it. Man, I got to get rid of that grain and empty my hide house. A fire-arrow in the roof and I'd lose it all."

"You may anyway," Brazos said and moved away from Ryker.

The two oldest Olroyd boys were fighting a horse while their father leaned against the wall and smoked

16

his pipe. He watched them with a certain detachment for he was a man who liked to see his sons work. Finally they brought the frightened horse under control and Jess Olroyd turned to Brazos.

"Seems you could find better horseflesh for a man; them Comanche ponies is plumb wild."

"Suppose you run down your own from now on," Brazos told him.

Olroyd grumbled something to himself and watched Jeb McClintock make a final inspection. Occasionally he sidled glances at Brazos Caine, slightly envious glances. Not a grateful man, Olroyd had to acknowledge that the settlement owed a great deal to Brazos Caine. Without him, they would have been without horses, for over a period of years the Mexicans and Comanches had stolen every horse in the settlement.

But Brazos Caine captured horses in the manner of the Comanches, by running them down until they were exhausted. Olroyd found it hard to credit a man with such physical prowess, but he had seen Brazos Caine do this, covering ground like a stag, then perhaps hours later leading the horse back, a braided grass rope over the lower jaw.

Jess Olroyd worried his back against the logs to relieve an itch. "Can't for the life of me see what all the hurry's about," he said.

McClintock looked around and paced the distance separating them. "Olroyd, you have talked against me enough. I'll have no more of it, do you understand?"

"I only spoke up when speakin' was called for," Oroyd said. "Guess I come near the truth, to get you so het up about it."

The others stopped what they were doing and observed this with some gravity. Olroyd saw that he had

17

an audience and decided to go one step further. "Appears to me that this is the time to talk some more. Jeb, you've been runnin' the settlement to suit yourself and I guess we been takin' it. I might be right when I say most of us are sick of it."

McClintock's eyes grew flinty and he darted a glance at Brazos Caine. "You been talkin' behind my back, boy?"

"No," Brazos said, "and don't accuse me of it either."

"I'll stand for no interference," McClintock said. "If you want my position, then earn it!"

"Didn't say I wanted it," Brazos told him. He glanced at the sky, noticing the solid layer of clouds hiding the sun. A ripe wind husked down off the far slopes. He sensed winter weather in the making, and in this country that meant torrential rains and driving winds and vast seas of mud. Pointing to the sky, he said, "Storm comin', Jeb. Be rainin' by morning."

McClintock favored the sky a brief glance, then grunted. "I've lived through storms before. You didn't answer me, boy."

"Do I have to?" Brazos asked. "Better watch the weather, Jeb. You can camp in a dry wash and in an hour be swimmin' a ragin' river that started as a flash flood twenty miles away."

For a moment McClintock considered this; he seemed like a father debating whether to whip the errant child or ignore him. When he reached his decision, he said, "Brazos Caine, as an officer of the Republic, I order you to join my command. For three years you have pulled against me, defied me, refused to work the land like the others. I've had enough! Don't make me put my hands on you in anger."

Stepping away from the wall, Brazos spoke softly.

18

"Never put your hands on me, McClintock. I wouldn't take kindly to it." He glanced at the others, then swung his eyes back to the old man. "The trouble with you people is, you're planters. Till th' land, you're always sayin'. Till, hell! You're fifty years early for that. The riches are on top of th' ground, was you sensible enough to see it."

"I'll have no rebellion from you or anyone else!" McClintock roared, his huge fists clenching. The women heard the commotion and crowded in Ryker's doorway to look. "You've plotted against me," McClintock accused. "I'll make a full report of this." He paused to search the faces around him. Some of them were for him, he knew, while others were against him, not openly, but against him nevertheless. "I see," he said, his anger making his voice low and rattling in his throat. "Did you all think I was simple-minded? That I haven't known what was goin' on?"

"Nothin's been goin' on," Ryker said from the doorway. "But some of us think Brazos is right. We'd be better off escortin' carts to Fort Davis than trying to fight Esqueda."

McClintock turned completely around while he spoke, "I've led you men since we all came to Texas. Led you well. Now you want to exchange *my* judgment for that of this—this Indian lover!"

"Careful now," Brazos warned. "Don't let your mouth get too big."

"By jumpin' Jesus!" McClintock bellowed. "It's time someone took you into hand!" He whirled and reached for the coiled whip on his saddle. With one flick he snaked it free.

"Mr. McClintock!" his wife said sharply. She tried to push past Ryker, but he held her back.

19

"This is man's business," Ryker said. "Best let them settle it."

Brazos Caine stood loose-muscled. He pointed to the whip. "I'd put that away if I was you. Flourish that at me and you'll have a fight on your hands."

"Fight? By Jesus, I'm giving you discipline!" He remembered Brazos' father standing by the wall and said, "Will I have to fight you too, Jubal?"

Jubal smiled in his beard and puffed his pipe. "You better handle him first—if you can."

McClintock's wrath exploded. He drew back his arm and the bullwhip whistled as it sailed back for the cast. Then Brazos Caine was on him like a mountain cat.

He caught the descending arm, whirled, and threw McClintock over his head. He struck the thick dust heavily, his breath pinched short by the sudden stop. Picking up the whip, Brazos chopped it into cordwood lengths with his bowie, then threw the pieces against the building. The old man lay where he had fallen. His wife rushed to him and tried to lift him, but McClintock's pride was strong and he struck her hands away. Getting painfully to his feet, he limped when he took an experimental step.

Brazos put his knife away and said, "That's a Comanche fighting trick. They'll teach you some others if you have a hand-to-hand brush with 'em." He moved his shoulders restlessly and his eyes flickered over the group. "I'll tell you once more; I'm goin' to Austin. I'll take you to Martin's place, but I know he won't go with you either."

He turned away as though nothing had happened and pushed his way into Ryker's store. Emma McClintock sat on his bale of beaver pelts and Brazos spoke softly. "You want me to say anything to Martin?"

20

"I said it last night," Emma said. "He's got to come to me. I ain't goin' to sneak around no more."

"He got you in trouble?"

Emma colored. "Nothin' like that. It just ain't fittin', that's all."

He left her and walked down the counter. Martha Olroyd was eating a slice of horn-cheese and a cracker. When Brazos looked at her he felt drawn toward her; she was like the call of a strange, far-off place, almost beyond resistance.

Martha studied him with a frankness that made him uneasy. Nodding to the front door, she said, "You've made an enemy out there."

"One more won't make any difference," he said and laughed. He laughed often and easily; in spite of his hard and dangerous life, Brazos Caine found much to give him pleasure. "McClintock's a stubborn fool who thinks he can walk over whoever he pleases."

"But not you, is that it?" She smiled. "Brazos, do you really want to take his place?"

"Not by a damn sight," he declared. "But he's old and touchy. Not much good any more."

"Harsh judgment," she said. "Ryker wants to see you take over, doesn't he?"

"Maybe. But I'm not goin' to." He sighed and swung his head to look out of the door. "I got troubles enough of my own."

"You better leave Emma alone," Martha advised. "I heard Zelia McClintock telling another woman that you've got Emma in a family way." She watched the quick color climb into his face.

"You're a fresh one, I declare," he said, "and I don't rightly know if I like it or not."

"You like it," she told him with calm assurance. "If

21

we were alone again I'll bet you'd try to kiss me."

He had the feeling that here was wisdom beyond him and he felt uneasy, clumsy. "Time to be goin'," he said and left the room, his moccasins sliding noiselessly across the dirt floor. Outside, McClintock was gathering his force and preparing to mount.

There was a flurry of movement at McClintock's command and the detail swung to the saddles. The leader sat his horse rifle-straight, his hair a flowing white mane across his shoulders. He wore no hat, considering it beneath his dignity to wear the wide sombrero like Ray Olroyd, or the Indian trappings of the Caines.

Ray Olroyd's horse turned skittish, and he let it prance until it was near the women, then racked sharply and lifted Emma McClintock off the ground. She cried out in surprise and anger and Ray kissed her before setting her down.

Jeb McClintock's face was like thunder and he wheeled his horse from the head and started back, but his son, Asa, copied Ray Olroyd and grabbed Martha. Brazos had watched Olroyd's maneuver with an amused detachment; but now he felt the sharp tug of anger and turned his horse also.

On his right, Antrim McClintock spoke softly. "Don't do anythin', Brazos."

His head whipped around and he found young Antrim relaxed on his horse, his cap-lock rifle negligently pointed at Brazos' stomach. Asa McClintock released Martha when she slapped him resoundingly, then rejoined the company.

"We'll march in a column of twos," McClintock said. "Forward!"

Antrim shifted his gun until the muzzle pointed up,

22

but still he watched Brazos. "Now don't get foxy with me," he said. "Brother Asa's had his eye on that for a smart spell. You better stay out of the hills unless you want to lose somethin'."

"Sure," Brazos said evenly and locked eyes with Antrim. The young man was not more than sixteen, but long a man in a land where manhood came with the ability to lift a rifle. "Sure, Antrim, but you point a gun at me again, you better shoot it."

"Maybe I will," Antrim said and Brazos rode to the head of the column. He turned in the saddle and looked back past the straggling group. Asa McClintock's face was wreathed in a smile and his eyes glittered with a triumph he did not bother to conceal. Ray Olroyd was riding beside Asa, a tall man with dark whiskers and a thin mouth. The two men talked in low tones, each bent toward the other until their heads almost touched.

Brazos settled in his saddle and worked this over in his mind. He did not pretend to understand Ray Olroyd, or Asa either. Nearly twenty, both men were wild and undisciplined and as lazy as pet coons. This last year, Olroyd had been taking to the hills more than usual, being gone for a week at a time. Several times Brazos had crossed his trail across the river, but had never seen him, which he considered strange, for Olroyd always rode a horse and a mounted man was easy to find.

Having the mountain man's natural disdain for riding, Brazos felt uncomfortable in the saddle. He rode poorly, he knew, and although he could have improved with practice, some innate stubbornness forbade his learning.

He glanced back once more at Asa McClintock and Ray Olroyd. Ray carried a Texas pistol tucked into his belt and Brazos wondered where he got it. In spite of their popularity with the regular militia, they were

23

expensive and hard to come by. He had had to journey all the way to New Orleans for his pair.

Yet Ray Olroyd plucked one out of the blue. Brazos Caine didn't understand this at all.

CHAPTER THREE

ONCE THE DETAIL PASSED OVER THE FIRST SMALL RISE, the settlement dropped from sight as though it had never existed, except in their minds. There had been no waving as the detachment rode out, no parting words, no gallant gestures. It did not occur to them to regard themselves as a band of heroes.

During the five years he had spent in Texas, Brazos Caine had come to accept danger as an everyday factor of existence and adjusted his life accordingly. His older brother, Penrod, had been the first to die; Brazos had found him hanging head down from a low branch, the fire that had roasted his brains long dead. Zack had been next; he had never been found.

With Brazos' younger sister it had started with the nohorn cow pulling her picket and straying past the barn. He had been with her when the bowstring twanged; even now he could hear the sodden impact of the arrow, her brief cry of pain, and then quite suddenly he and his father and mother were alone in the world.

Actually he was not alone, for the others carried with them the memory of death. There was no safety here, no task secure from the Comanches and the raiding Mexicans. Milking contained certain risks, for the Comanches soon learned this routine and lay in wait with a savage patience.

Before the first year had passed, Brazos Caine

24

decided that survival lay in a man's ability to best the enemy at his own game, so he began patiently to develop his skills until he surpassed the Indians he fought. From Martin, Brazos learned the fine points of tracking and Martin was grateful for this ally who chose to live as he lived. Yet there was a difference. Brazos did not possess Martin's dark and brooding hatred for Comanche, Apache and Mexican.

In the beginning, they made raids against the Comanches, sneaking into their camps, and making off with horses. Then Brazos' skill and daring grew, and he went out alone, laying traps, frustrating war parties until his name and his prowess were balefully uttered watchwords among the Comanches.

There was a price to be paid for this hard-won knowledge, a price that set Brazos Caine apart from other men. More and more, Brazos found the gulf widening between him and the settlers at Ryker's. A man who lives with the wilderness becomes slightly wild, slightly undisciplined and unpredictable, and men look for the predictable in their neighbor. This was not his wish, for Brazos was a man who needed other men around him. He needed a woman too.

I'll speak of it to Martha when I return, he thought.

McClintock led the party in a long, roundabout route that followed the bluffs overlooking the Rio Grande. Toward evening they reached the crest of a long hill that let down into the ragged valley separating two small ranges. Other hills lay ahead of them, higher and more forbidding, each holding its own unseen danger.

The mountains rose in a rough ring around this narrow valley and the column moved at a leisurely walk, pausing when full darkness caught them in a deeply wooded glen between two hogbacks.

25

Ryker's settlement was nearly twenty miles to the west now.

McClintock dismounted and saddle leather protested. "Camp here," he said, indicating a spot where brush grew thick and the grass was belly-deep to a horse.

Glancing around, Brazos said, "Poor place, Jeb. Be better to push on to Martin's place. Only ten more miles."

McClintock came over to Brazos' horse. "What's wrong with this? There's fuel and shelter."

Brazos' shoulders rose and fell gently. "Poor place to defend, down in a hollow like this. If it rains tonight, you'll swim."

There was no give in McClintock's face. "Appears to me that all you Indian lovers are full of supposin's and maybe's and if's. Now I gave an order. Dismount and build a fire. We got to eat."

"Fire?" Brazos slid from his pony. "Don't build a fire. The risk's too great."

There was a long pause, then McClintock spoke to his son without turning his head. "Asa, gather some wood and build a fire." He turned to the Olroyds and began ordering them to a dozen tasks. Brazos watched this for a moment, then led his horse to a spot thirty yards distant and made his picket. From his possible sack, Brazos produced cold jerky and corn meal. He ate this cold and watched McClintock's glowing fire. The odor of cooked meat grew strong on the wind and, after they had finished, Ray Olroyd and Asa McClintock came over, squatting by Brazos. The night was a sooty thickness between them and the two men were vague shapes in the grass.

Asa McClintock said softly, "You ain't pecked at me, are you, Brazos?"

26

"Should I be?"

"She ain't yours," Asa said somewhat stiffly.

"I know that," Brazos said. "If she was you'd still be layin' in front of Ryker's."

The bluntness stopped Asa for a moment, then he looked over his shoulder at the fire. "You don't like that?"

"No skin off me," Brazos said. He plucked a blade of grass and began to chew it. "A man don't stay in one place in Indian country, not if he's got a lick of sense. Keep movin', that's best. If you got to camp at all, then camp high and cold." He switched his head back and forth like a dog sniffing the breeze. "Can't see a goddamned thing in this hollow. If they come in awhoopin', they'd cut us to hell before we got to the rim. Be no ridin' out either, because they'd get us from the top. A man'd have to go straight up the doggoned sides."

Asa laughed uneasily. "Hell, there ain't no Comanches around here."

"Think not?" Brazos let the silence fill up. "They're watchin' all the time; every damned move we make, they watch. Away from the settlement you got to sleep with an eye open and your rifle cocked."

Ray Olroyd didn't like this. "You think they watched us leave Ryker's?"

"It's possible," Brazos admitted and settled back on his sleeping robe. "Anything's possible in Indian country."

"I've been meanin' to talk to you," Ray Olroyd said, squatting on his haunches. "Made a few trips out myself, but there's a lot I don't know about trappin'. I thought maybe you and me could work together the next time you go."

"I don't like partners," Brazos said.

"Make you a good man," Olroyd said, smiling. "I ain't hard to get along with."

"But I am," Brazos said. "You seem to be doin' all right. You got yourself a Colt's pistol, didn't you?"

"Why—I picked it off'n a Mexican I killed a while back. What's wrong with that?"

"Nothin', if it's the way you say." He turned his head as Jeb McClintock stood against the remaining light of the fire, a tall, black outline. McClintock flipped his head around and peered through the darkness at Brazos' cold camp. A moment later he came over.

"Stubborn as a jackass," McClintock said.

"You wanted me along because I know Indians," Brazos said. "All right. I gave you advice and you ignored it. Now do as you damn please."

Surprisingly, the old man showed no resentment. He stroked his whiskers and asked, "How far did you say it was to Martin's place?"

"An easy ride if you're careful."

"You'll scout it?"

"I said I would." He stood up and began to gather his robes and to pack parfleche. "Asa, you lead my horse while I go ahead on foot."

McClintock returned to the fire and ordered it put out. Men moved quickly, assembling their gear, and were soon mounted. Ray Olroyd edged close to Brazos and said, "I meant what I said; I'd like to go with you."

"Go by yourself," Brazos told him bluntly. "I ain't showin' my traps to no man. Was I to see you in that country, I'd leave a ball in you for the buzzards to pick out."

"May be the other way around one of these days," Olroyd said and moved away.

McClintock came up. "Your damned talk of Indians has got me jumpy."

"You should be jumpy," Brazos said. "They'll find the remains of the fire before morning." He checked the caps on his five-shot Colt's pistols, then added, "I'll take a twenty yard lead," before turning and moving out, his head bent to study the dark ground.

The night was ink, with the clouds gathered in thick masses and the wind moaning softly through the tall grass. Leading them out of the draw, Brazos Caine took to the ridges, following them unerringly although he could see no more than twenty paces ahead.

Behind him the detail strung out for a hundred yards, curb chains rattling and harness protesting. He halted and passed the word back to muffle equipment. The saddles were the heavy Mexican variety with huge roll on the cantle and pommel. The bits were chain with forge-welded links. Brazos showed them how to fasten a loop of rein around the lower jaw, thereby getting rid of the bits entirely.

With this done, he moved out again, head back, swinging it from side to side to catch any movement, any scent that would give him a split-second advantage over the enemy. He knew the night and the tricks it could play on a man's vision. By keeping his eyes in constant motion, he could pick out movement more quickly with the edge of his vision than by a steady stare.

In spite of the darkness, there was always enough light to study the ground, and he did this, moving with his head down at times. The slick side of the grass reflects light, but when there has been an impress made on it, or if grass is bent, then it shows darker, a vague shadow that tells a story.

Suddenly he paused to kneel. Ahead, a dark spot indicated grass that had been bent flat and, as he watched, these spots popped erect. McClintock came up and opened his mouth to speak, but Brazos raised a hand for silence. After waiting a moment, he said, "Let's go now."

"Is it safe?" McClintock asked.

"You're never safe, but it'll be better if we're moving."

He started out again, the others following, leading their horses.

For two hours he set a steady pace, not stopping or allowing anyone to mount. When he halted, he did so so abruptly that the others bunched around him. Motioning for them to squat, he waited until they did, then pointed to several mounted shadows scudding over a ridge not more than fifty yards away. A horse pulled in a lungful of air and Brazos bowled Jeb McClintock over to clap a hand over the flared nostrils. The tight fingers shut off the whinny before it started and Brazos waited until the horse gave up the idea before releasing her.

Realizing how close they had come to detection, McClintock said, "Get us to Martin's, for Christ sake!"

Near midnight they raised the low shadow of Martin's cabin and out-buildings. McClintock was in favor of mounting and riding in, Brazos restrained him. "At night he wouldn't be able to tell you from Mexicans. I'll belly up and signal him. When he puts on a light, come in quiet and turn the animals into the shelter back of the lean-to." Brazos put his hand on McClintock's arm. "From here, head straight for Martin's door. He's got bear traps hid all over the yard. You stay in a straight line and you'll miss 'em. This is the only way in without gettin' caught."

Approaching Martin's cabin carefully, Brazos worried some about the Comanches that had paced the column since leaving Ryker's. Although he had only come in contact with them during the last few hours, he felt sure that they had been with McClintock's force during the entire journey. Like most frontiersmen, Brazos did not worry about this so much as he did the questions such actions raised in his mind. The Comanches had not closed in and they should have. He could not understand their failure to attack.

The fact that the Indians had moved off told Brazos that the Comanche leader had guessed their destination to be Martin's. Bellying up through the short grass, Brazos whistled.

For a moment there was nothing, then the shadows around Martin's heavy door deepened as it opened a crack. A rifle barrel protruded a few inches. Brazos closed the distance to twenty yards and Martin asked, *"Qué desea usted ?"*

"Martin!" Brazos whispered through cupped hands.

"Esta' bueno," Martin said and a moment later a candle flared from within, a dirty yellow light seeping through the fleshed buffalo-hide windows. Brazos ran back to where the others waited and led them along an unmarked path. Near the cabin he said, "Go straight to the lean-to." Martin had come out and stood in the darkness, his Colt's revolving rifle cradled in the crook of his arm.

Martin was a man in his late twenties, a short man with a bull-neck and a barrel-chest. His arms were short and powerful. He wore greasy buckskins, almost skin tight, and he never took them off, save once a year when a Mexican woman at Fort Davis or San Felipe de Austin made him a new pair. There was a wildness about

31

Martin that was lacking in Brazos, and this was not merely a matter of years spent in the wilderness. The reason lay bedded in Martin's thinking, for he had almost completely shed the white man's ways.

Pushing past Brazos, McClintock entered the cabin. The solitary candle on the table cast a feeble light and he looked around at the dirt floor, the grass mattress covered with a cowhide. He disapproved of this, for he believed that a white man should live better, simply because he was white.

Glancing at Olroyd's three sons, and at the others crowding his cabin door, Martin asked, "Goin' possum huntin'?"

"We're organized militia," McClintock said sternly, "and our intention is to eliminate Esqueda and his followers."

"With this bunch?" Martin laughed. He turned to the mantel for his pipe and crushed shag tobacco into it, then bent over the candle for his light.

He puffed until his face was wreathed in smoke. Martin was a strange man, not readily understood by these people, and they were uncomfortable around him. Many were afraid of him; he had once killed another man over a trifle. He spoke little and asked for nothing, offering friendship to Brazos and no other. Most of the time Martin was in the hills; even when he returned to the settlement with his pelts, he did not stay long, and if he did, he would quarrel.

Moving away from the table, Martin asked, "The Comanches quiet?" His face was dark and his beard stubble made a bluish cast to his square jaw.

"They appear to be," McClintock admitted. "Saw some roamin' around as we came over. The first I seen in three months."

"That's the time to worry, when you can't see 'em." He waved his pipe at the group waiting just outside. "I gather that you want me along. Is that right, McClintock?"

"I had that in mind, yes." The old man seemed relieved that he did not have to ask.

"I wouldn't go," Martin said flatly. "Brazos and I are goin' to Austin. You want to gad around and get killed, then go ahead."

McClintock decided not to argue but he could not resist an opportunity to speak his mind. "Seems strange to me," he said, "that you can live here alone and be gone half the time and yet have no Indians botherin' you."

Martin took his pipe from his mouth and looked intently at McClintock. "I was burned out once. I trailed that Comanche for seventy miles before I caught him, then I worked on him with my knife. It took him nine days to die and then I dumped him near his village. That keeps 'em away, mister. They know what'll happen if I take out after 'em."

Here was the facet of Martin's make-up that McClintock could not comprehend. This savageness, so alien to a white man, offended McClintock. He could kill, but to commit atrocities was beyond his understanding.

"You'd be valuable to me, should you come along," McClintock said. "I have a sound plan. We intend to ambush Esqueda when he crosses the river near the mission. Fortified in the rocks, we will have a strong position."

Martin disagreed with a shake of his head. "Kind of a fight. Esqueda knows best, the ambush."

"Man," McClintock urged, "Esqueda killed your

brother. I thought you'd like to—"

"In my own way," Martin interrupted. "Not with this ragtail bunch behind me." He waved his hand absently. "Help yourselves to whatever shelter you can find. There's cut grass in the lean-to for pallets and if you step into a trap out there, it's your own tough luck."

McClintock motioned to his men and they walked around the cabin. He lingered in the doorway. "Where do I sleep?"

"Outside."

"That's not what I call friendly," he said.

"Who the hell wants to be friendly with you?" Martin said. "I'm not good enough for the McClintocks; you made that plain to me once. Now sleep with the horses."

Puffing his cheeks, McClintock seemed on the verge of an explosion, but wheeled and went outside. From behind the cabin, small noises filtered through as the men bedded down for the night.

Brazos pulled a low, split-log stool away from the table and sat down. Martin kindled a fire and hooked a bucket on the fireplace crane. He squatted before the blaze, not speaking until the coffee was done.

"What about them Indians you saw?" he asked, then turned his head to look at Brazos.

He told Martin about the fire and the fresh sign. The coffee was done and Martin lifted the bucket with a poker. He muffled this in a rag and poured a tin cup full. "Take it," he said. "I'll drink from the bucket."

They nursed the strong brew in silence, then Martin asked, "Ever seen Esqueda?"

Brazos shook his head. "McClintock had his trouble with him before I come here." He paused to shave some tobacco into his coffee, then stirred it with the blade of his knife. "You was here before that, Martin. You seen

34

him, ain't you?"

"Not a big man," Martin said as though he had a special reason for remembering. "Wears a fancy jacket with a lot of silver trimmin'. Must be twenty dollars worth there." He finished his coffee and shied the grounds into the fireplace. "Emma have any word for me?"

"She says she ain't goin' to sneak off no more," Brazos said.

Martin sat motionless for a moment. "Th' damn little snip! Workin' her sly ways, that's what she's doin'. She knows I think of her some. A man gets tired of some squaw on a blanket. He gets to wantin' a white woman and she knows it."

"It's your problem," Brazos said. "I'm not fixin' up any more meetin's between you two." He finished his coffee and shoved the tin cup away. "But I think I got it figured out."

"What figured out?"

"Them Comanches we saw tonight." He sat upright, his eyes shining. "They were scouts, as sure as I'm settin' here. Likely as not Ryker's will be burned to the ground by the time Old Iron Pants gets back from his turkey hunt. It's been botherin' me that Esqueda ain't made another raid lately and now I guess I know why. He's wanted to get McClintock and a party away from the settlement; then he could take it all without gettin' his men shot up."

"He's got to cross the river," Martin said.

"Yeah," Brazos admitted, "that's bothered me some; how he was goin' to do that, but I got that figured too. He's across now! Probably camped some place on this side, him and his Comanches, just waitin' and watchin'."

Martin slapped his palms together. "By Jesus, you could be right!" He turned and crossed to his bunk. "I'll throw a parfleche together and we'll head out. If there is a ruckus and we can get through with a warnin', they might hold 'em off."

"You think McClintock will believe me and come back?"

"Who gives a damn? I just want a shot at that Mexican!"

CHAPTER FOUR

MARTIN ROLLED HIS SLEEPING ROBE AND TIED IT, THEN buckled on his pistol belt. At this time few men carried their handguns in hip scabbards, this being pretty much a Texas innovation. Since the dawn of pistol carrying, men tucked them into belts or special saddle holsters, but the Texans needed their guns quickly and soon the hip holster came into popularity.

By frontier standards, Martin was not heavily armed, although he had his five-shot Colt's pistol and an eightshot .44 Colt's rifle, plus his Green River knife. Slinging his war bag to his shoulder, Martin crossed to the door as Brazos blew out the candle and followed him around the side of the building.

McClintock raised himself on one elbow as they stopped by the first lean-to. He saw Martin rigged for traveling and said, "What in thunderation is this?"

"We're goin' back to Ryker's," Brazos said and gave his reasons.

"This is mutiny!" McClintock said, his bull voice arousing the others.

"This is sense," Brazos insisted. "Besides, we both

36

said we wasn't comin' with you. Now you can come back with us or get yourself killed. I'd advise you to saddle up and follow us as soon as you can."

"I'll have you both flogged for this!" McClintock threatened. "You're defyin' my orders." He shook a finger at Brazos. "I see through your scheme. You want to make me turn back because I'll have no scout and in that way weaken me by making me ridiculous before the people."

"You damn fool," Brazos said. "Esqueda's on this side right now."

"Agh," the old man said, "I think, I guess, if—ain't you sure of anything?"

"No more'n you are," Brazos said. "I'll leave my horse and go afoot with Martin. Follow as quick as you can and if you stay to the ridges you'll make it with your hair."

McClintock tried to compromise. "Can't we wait 'til mornin' ?"

"Night's the best time for travelin'," Brazos said. "The Comanches know where we are now and like as not know what we're up to. I think they'll hit Ryker's around daylight. If you're ready to move now, we could be there in time."

"Stop guessin' and give me facts," McClintock complained. "I'm a military man and a fact is somethin' I understand."

"I'll be a horse's ass," Martin said and turned away in disgust.

"We're goin'," Brazos said and McClintock threw aside his robe and stood up.

He turned with Martin and moved into the darkness. McClintock's voice followed them. "By the Prophet, I'll come back just to strip the skin off your damn backs!"

37

But Brazos and Martin had already melted into the night and were halfway across the clearing. Brazos set the pace, a loose, jogging mile-eater.

At the end of an hour they had traveled five miles, and overhead the clouds sported breaks in their solid surface, allowing a feeble moonlight to dribble through. Sweat was a-shine on their faces as they ran.

For a brief moment they flopped belly-flat in the grass and rested although neither was breathing hard. Finally Brazos said, "Let's go," and struck out unerringly in the darkness. They ran without sound, their moccasins parting the grass with barely a whisper.

For another hour they moved west by north, then Brazos said, "That's where I saw 'em." He indicated the rise of ground where the Comanche scouts had been.

Nodding, Martin cut down into the draw, skirting the south slope and, under this cover, moved a little faster. They ran with long-legged strides, in an effortless drive that saved wind. Within the hour, Martin found the remains of McClintock's fire as certainly as if he himself had made it. Brazos knelt and examined the ashes, then stood up and said, "They've been here, all right." He glanced around and the ridges stood out darkly against the night sky. The clouds were a rolling mass now anti a new, stronger wind bent the grass in an undulating wave. "You can leave your pack here," he said. "They won't come back."

"We've been makin' time," Martin admitted, once his breathing had quieted. Sweat ran in streaks down his face and he smelled strongly of wood smoke and sharp animal odors. "I just hope Iron Pants don't walk them damned horses," he added.

"Don't count on it," Brazos said and knelt again. "Been over four hours since the Comanches were here.

We got to make better time, for they'll be ringin' Ryker's by mornin'." He glanced at the sky. "Three hours left, maybe a little more. Another eighteen miles. You got the wind for it?"

"I'm all right," Martin said and indicated that he was ready to move out. Brazos started off with a lengthened pace, Martin at his heels, the long muscles of his legs pulling and driving like pistons.

Together, they ran on into the night.

Without the bulky parfleche, Martin found running easier and he matched Brazos' strides. Their breathing deepened and perspiration ran in rivulets down their faces. After an hour of this muscles began to burn and Brazos' nose commenced bleeding as he drove himself to the limit of his endurance. He scudded along a ridge, his head continually swinging. The smell of rain seemed stronger now and the sky boiled. To the east, lightning made ragged streaks of light in the heavens while thunder boomed seconds later.

Brazos stopped quickly as he saw something in the grass. Martin knelt beside him and Brazos examined the horse droppings. "Two hours or thereabouts," he said and began to run again. This he had learned from the Apaches, who trained their children in the tracking art. An old Apache, wise in the way of the land, would gather a bag of droppings and ride some faint trail, scattering them from time to time. The children, trailing, had to learn to tell how old the dropping was by breaking it and observing the thickness of the dried crust.

Such a thing would never occur to a white man, that this offal could talk, but to the plainsman it told a complete story. Time of passage for the horse. Range-fed or grain-fed, and if grain, perhaps a soldier's horse,

39

a friend or enemy, depending on who read the sign.

Through the last of the night and into the first grayness of a stormy dawn the men ran on. As the sky lightened, their vision extended to the next ridge of hills. Brazos forged ahead now, driving himself to even greater speed. His hair lay in a wet pattern over his forehead. Sweat had soaked through his buckskins until they clung skin-tight. His legs were pumping rhythmically and his nosebleed had stopped. His arms, driving forward with each stride, added power and gave him speed.

Neither of these men would have been able to say how they could run at this speed for so great a distance; theirs was the stamina of wild game, developed by necessity in a land that held no mercy for the weak. All their lives they had been running for one reason or another, often in fun, but at other times, simply to stay alive.

Skirting the sharp backbone of a ridge, they ran along the edge, low enough to be shielded from the lightening sky. Then Brazos flopped down, breathing through his open mouth. Martin crouched beside him.

Ryker's settlement lay in the broad valley below them, peaceful in the first light. But it was a false peace; on the other ridge, Comanche warriors waited, invisible to the settlement, but in sight of the two men lying in the grass.

There was no sign of activity around the settlement buildings. Brazos' string of two-wheeled carts still stood in Indian file behind the lean-to sheds, resting forward on dropped tongues. Several horses stirred in another shed, but all was quiet.

"They got no way of knowin'," Brazos said. "There must be someone on guard." He paused to wipe sweat from his face. "Hell of a lot of good that'll do when them Comanches come off that hill." He searched the land ahead of them, especially the down-tilted slope that led into the settlement. "Think there's anybody out there?"

"Don't know," Martin said softly.

Both men studied an Indian on the far ridge.

The Comanche was a proud warrior, fierce, courageous, and extremely daring. He sat his horse arrowstraight, buckskin-clad legs wrapped around the animal's barrel. The Comanches were, on the average, less than tall, when judged by a white man's standards. They wore their hair long and braided with muskrat pelts until a streamer of hair and fur fell from ear to waist. Their breastplates were drilled bone and lay flat like a vest. Some wore the full war bonnet of feathers and their horses were painted with broad stripes, jagged streaks or circle drawings with huge dots in the center like a target.

Brazos touched Martin and pointed to an Indian at the crest of the far rise. "Met him before. That's Ten Bears, a big chief." He got to his hands and knees. "If we're goin', now's the time."

"It's better'n a mile," Martin said doubtfully. "Can we run it?"

"The only way," Brazos said. "Likely Ten Bears has warriors strung out in the grass below. We'll have to go smack-dab through 'em so run with your pistol in one hand and your knife in the other. Should I go down, don't stop. I won't stop for you."

"Let's go," Martin said and freed his revolving pistol. They lived by the hard code of survival. To pause and help a downed man might bring death to both, and in this land, one more rifle or pistol could change defeat

41

into victory.

Brazos drew his pistol from the holster on his right hip and cocked it. The folding trigger popped out and he kept his finger away from it lest the jar waste a shot. When both had their pistols and knives in hand, Brazos rose quickly and they broke off the slope together, running downhill.

Martin had his rifle slung across his back and his accoutrements bobbed crazily as he followed Brazos in long jumps. The knee-length grass afforded little cover now so they kept to the shrubs as much as possible, hoping to blend in. They ran without noise, making good speed. They had traveled half the distance when a warrior gave a shout and a bowstring twanged.

From the grass ahead, three Comanches rose swiftly and notched arrows to their bows. The distance was close, not more than fifty yards, and closing rapidly. Raising his pistol, Brazos fired without breaking stride and the huge Texas Colt recoiled and belched smoke. One brave was flung completely around by the ball and twitched a moment before falling limply.

Another brave launched an arrow that missed before Brazos raised his gun, sighted quickly through the notched hammer lip and shot. The Comanche spun away with a shattered pelvis.

A ringing whoop went up on the other hillside and the air was suddenly filled with shouting braves and the drum of running horses. The distance between the two men and the remaining braves was dangerously close and the Comanche discarded his bow for a scalping knife. He made a lunging pass at Brazos, who flung the Indian aside and continued on at a dead run.

Ryker's settlement was coming awake now and the sound of gunfire bucketed against the hills as the

Comanches under Ten Bears tried to come across the gully and support their fellow warriors. Rifles were thrust through the narrow battlement slits, picking out targets. To the left and right of Brazos and Martin, more Comanches rose from concealment and tried to converge, but the distance was too great. The running men were far ahead.

Around the battlements powder smoke made a thin cloud as men fired and reloaded. From the number of rifles firing out of Ryker's, Brazos judged that the women were shooting also.

The brave Brazos had knocked asprawl was trying to rise when Martin bore down on him. He skewered the Comanche on the ten-inch blade of his Green River knife yanking it free without breaking his stride.

Then suddenly, strangely, Martin halted and went back to where the dead Comanche lay. Brazos, seeing this maneuver in a back-glance, turned and came back too. Martin had laid aside his pistol and was lifting the Comanche's hair.

"You damn savage!" Brazos yelled and picked up Martin's Colt. The mounted warriors of Ten Bears were less than two hundred yards away now and coming on at a gallop. Martin, bent over the Indian, made a small slit high on the forehead, then reversed his knife and made two backward cuts. He lifted the scalplock with a sharp sucking sound.

An arrow thudded into the ground not three feet from him, but he did not even look up. Brazos was kneeling and sighting Martin's pistol. It roared and recoiled and a horse faltered, then went into a stumbling roll. He shot again, and again, without apparent effect; his fourth shot knocked a brave to the ground.

Suddenly Martin began firing his repeating rifle. He was prone behind the body of the Indian and his eyes were squinted over the long octagonal barrel. Two more ponies were without riders when Ten Bears shouted and the charge broke away on a running tangent.

High on a near hill, a man wheeled his white horse and a trumpet sounded, a sharp ringing above the boom of guns. The Comanches withdrew to reorganize and Brazos began to run toward the settlement again. He turned his head once to see if Martin was still behind him and when he did, he saw the morning light reflect from the silver on the mounted man's jacket.

"Esqueda," he said, almost reverently.

Reorganized now, Ten Bears led his remaining braves in a last attempt to cut Brazos and Martin off before they reached the settlement, but their lead was a good one and they ran like deer.

Martin was running with a rifle in one hand, his empty pistol in the other. The bleeding scalplock was clenched tightly between his teeth and his wind whistled through his nose as he ran.

The pursuing Indians were firing their muskets with little effect. With their arrows they could hit a running antelope at seventy yards, but their muskets were clumsily handled and ineffective.

Brazos and Martin had a hundred and fifty yards lead but the mounted Comanches were closing the distance. As Brazos began the last sprint toward Ryker's door, the rifles from the loopholes spoke and a wave of shouting rose from the Comanches.

Ten Bears yelled at his braves, urging them on, for ahead was Sun-in-the-Hair, who had slain many Comanches. Rifles again spoke from the embrasures and Ten Bears veered to the left, leaving three downed men behind. Ryker had the door open as they neared the settlement and Brazos fell back, allowing Martin to enter first.

As Martin cleared the threshold, an arching arrow found him and drove him staggering into the building. He dropped his rifle and pistol and sat down heavily, the scalplock still clenched between his teeth.

Ryker slammed the door and slid the ash bar in place. Brazos squatted on the dirt floor, pulling in great gulps of air as the firing began with renewed thunder. Someone in the room yelled and then began to moan.

Outside, the Comanches were streaming down the hillside in another desperate attack; inside was Sun-in-the-Hair, killer of Comanches, and savage blood cried out for vengeance. Brazos looked at Martin, then reached out and snatched the lice-ridden scalplock away from him, throwing it in the corner. "Don't ever pull another stunt like that on me again, Martin!"

"No—one made—you stop," Martin said, glancing at the arrow through his side. The shaft had pierced the muscle, missing the organs, and he grasped it behind the head and pulled it through.

Clasping a hand over the wound, he sat there cursing while blood seeped through his tight-pressed fingers. Someone stirred beside him and he turned slightly. Emma McClintock stared at him, wide-eyed.

Ryker's building was beginning to get hazy with powder smoke and the firing went on, a dull rattle that was muffled by the thick walls. The Comanches rode back and forth across the face of the settlement, pouring in musket balls and arrows with little effect.

Leaving Martin on the floor, Brazos went to the bar where his father fired from a loophole below a bullhide window. Musket balls thudded into the walls and Jubal Caine took a running aim on a brave, shot, and watched him cascade from his horse.

"Where's the others?" he asked.

"Martin's place, when we left," Brazos said and thrust his pistol through another loophole, then withdrew it when he saw that the range was too great. Jubal sat with a mouth full of buckskin patches, chewing them while he poured powder down the barrel, or removed a ball from his shot pouch. Spitting out a patch, he rammed it home, capped the gun and waited for a decent target.

"The others comin' in or goin' on?"

"Maybe they'll come in," Brazos said. "Old Iron Pants can't find his ass with both hands and he knows it."

Jubal grunted, then nodded toward the other room. "Martin hit?"

"He'll live through it," Brazos said and watched the Comanches gather on the hillside. "Emma's with him, as if he needed her."

"She his woman?" When Brazos gave him a glance and no answer, Jubal added, "Too bad. She ain't built for a youngun a year, but he won't care. He'll see that he don't miss his fun." He shook his head. "Too damn bad."

From the other wall, Jess Olroyd's gun made a steady boom, then he yelled, "That was no goddamned Comanche ! I just shot me a Mexican!" He swiveled his head toward Jubal. "You see that?"

From the entire front of the settlement rifles coughed bluntly, paused, then spoke again. With the hillside buttressing Ryker's from the back, the Comanches had to concentrate their attack on three sides, making

46

impossible their favorite tactic, circling. The Indians stayed well away from the settlement now for the cap-lock rifle was deadly at two hundred yards.

Martin came into the room, his side bandaged. He took a position at one of the loopholes and waited. Emma squatted beside him, and Brazos found himself wishing she wouldn't do that. Martin would be flattered for a while, but after her newness wore off, he'd likely cuff her out of the way; he was a man who tired of a thing quickly.

Somewhere upstairs a rifle banged. Outside the full dawn light bloomed into a gray day and the clouds hung low, rolling, rain-filled and threatening to spill over at any time.

Looking through the loophole at the hills, Brazos could see no sight of McClintock and the others. This worried him for Emiliano Esqueda knew how feebly the settlement was defended and would keep up the attack until he was victorious.

The rifle spoke again upstairs and Jubal Caine said, "Better get up there. Martha's alone."

"The little snip," Brazos said and went up the stairs.

CHAPTER FIVE

THE FOUR FRONT ROOMS SAT FLUSH WITH THE FACE of the settlement and Brazos Caine went into the center one when he heard the dull pop of the rifle. He found Martha Olroyd kneeling by an opening in the embrasure. She turned her tow head and gave him a wide smile as he squatted beside her. Her face was smudged with burnt powder and one of her braids had come undone, allowing her hair to fall loosely over one

47

shoulder.

"I saw your run," she said. "Just like a deer without horns."

"If that's the way a deer feels," Brazos said, "I'll swear off huntin'." He moved her to one side and squinted through the rifle port. The Comanches were parading back and forth across the breast of the hill, shouting and waving their decorated lances. Esqueda's white horse stood out sharply against the sunless sky and darkly swollen rain clouds.

Martha held her Hawken rifle across her lap, her palms blackened from handling the fouled ramrod. When she raised her hand to brush hair away from her forehead, she left another smudge above her eyebrows.

"Too far away for a shot," Brazos said tightly. "That Esqueda's a smart bast—fella."

"They're not shooting any more," she said and leaned back against the wall. He glanced at her and decided that she was still pretty as a fuzzy pup, even with the smudges on her face. Pretty, and very hard to know . . . last year he had tried to kiss her and had been slapped soundly; after that he had left her alone but he remained painfully conscious of her charms . . .

"They don't have to shoot," Brazos said. "They got us in a bind and Esqueda knows it."

"Are my brothers alive?" She kept the worry out of her voice, but it was there in her eyes.

"When I last seen 'em, they was," he told her and put his face to the rifle port again. A small band of Comanches broke away from the main body and tried to angle around on the flank to fire the lean-tos, but someone below shot a brave from his pony and the entire group wheeled and rode back up the hillside.

"No sense of worryin'," Brazos said. "McClintock

48

will be along soon."

"You don't really believe that." She closed her eyes and listened to the Comanches yell. The warriors still paraded back and forth across the hillside, shouting at the settlement, taunting and threatening.

Martha listened to this for several minutes, then clapped her hands over her ears and snapped, "Why do they have to yell?" She took a firmer grip of herself and slanted Brazos a glance that was half ashamed. "Why did you come back? I thought you were going to San Felipe de Austin."

It was in his mind to tell her that the thought of her blond hair decorating some Comanche's lance had pulled him back, but he reckoned he wasn't on that kind of a footing with her. "A man gets a feelin' to do somethin' and he does it, that's all."

"I went outside after a bucket of water a while ago," Martha said. "Emma was moonin' over Martin. He goin' to take her as his woman?"

"I don't know," Brazos said. "It's his business, whatever he does." He shot her an amused glance. "I swear, you're th' nosiest woman I ever saw." He laughed softly, then stopped to listen. Outside the Comanches still rode back and forth but were careful to stay out of range; already a dozen were dead or wounded. Brazos saw a score of Mexicans who had now discarded their Indian disguises; Esqueda himself had withdrawn to a higher promontory where he could command a sweeping view of the land.

But the Comanche gibberish had not caught Brazos' trained ears. He cocked his head to one side and heard a splatter of rain falling on the roof; then it increased to a full rattle, drowning out the other sounds.

"No fire-arrows now," he said and leaned back

49

against the wall, tired but content. His legs and back ached from his exertions earlier, but he ignored this minor discomfort. The rifle fire from the besieged settlement dropped off to nothing, but each man clung to his loophole for this was only a matter of waiting now.

A glance through the firing slot assured Brazos that Esqueda was laying siege and that there would be no letup of the fight, for tonight, or in the morning, it would be renewed. The Comanches dismounted from their ponies and squatted on the ground, their heavy blankets around them. The slanting rain reduced visibility but Brazos could distinguish them on the far hillside, waiting with savage patience.

Martha Olroyd sat with her shoulder touching his. He glanced at her and found her studying her hands. She had a round face, her nose was straight and her lips were full and expressive. He had never forgotten that one brief touch of her lips

Martha asked, "What kind of a man is Martin, Brazos?"

"A good man," Brazos said.

"A good man to have in the hills, or good in his heart?"

"I don't know anything about his heart," he said, "or anybody else's."

"It's always seemed strange to me that you and him got along," she said softly. "There's gentleness in you, Brazos, but he's—wild. Like some animal turned loose. I saw him running with that scalp in his teeth. Why does he hate so? Because of his brother?"

"I guess."

"I don't believe that, Brazos," she said with a shake of her head. "He's paid the Comanches back, but that hasn't satisfied him. It's his excuse for bein' what he is.

He's burning up inside with hate. Hate for everything he sees."

"Not for Emma," Brazos contradicted. "He wants her."

"Emma's not what he wants," Martha said. "He hates Jeb McClintock and he'll get at him through Emma."

This surprised Brazos, although the thought had been in his own mind. He glanced at her again and his eyes focused on her lips—full, warm lips that drove strange yearnings through him. She shifted against him, stretching her legs out before her. Her body was full; he could see the rounded outlines of her legs through the coarse homespun of her dress.

He thought about the many times he had watched the unconscious sway of her hips when she walked, then frowned when he recalled Asa McClintock and his sharp eyes leering in the same direction. Asa was aware of her too, Brazos concluded, for Martha would fit a man's bed; she was that kind, with a natural zest for life that whetted male desires.

Martha's soft voice brought his attention back. "You thinking about kissing me?"

"That was the furthest thing from my mind!" Brazos said guiltily, his face going red to the roots of his hair.

"The brave deserve a kiss," Martha told him, an odd stirring in her voice. She said it as though she were restraining herself, and he stood up, pulling her to her feet. The warmth of her body drove through his buckskins, making his heart pound erratically. When she gave him her lips he intended to be rough to show her his full male appetite, but something restrained him and he found himself growing weak until it was she who controlled this thing. He forgot to breathe but that did not matter; only that their lips did not part mattered. She pulled away at last and laid her head against him, her arms tight around his waist.

"I made up my mind when I seen you runnin'," she said softly. "Brazos, the risks you take, I just can't take the chance on waitin'."

"Beats me why you slapped my face that time," he said. "I sure bet you never slapped Asa McClintock that hard."

Smiling, Martha took his face between her palms and gave him a long kiss. "A little waiting makes it better, don't it?"

"By golly, you're a smart one," Brazos admitted. "I'll have to watch that after I marry you." He frowned; he was getting ahead of himself. "You will marry me, won't you?"

"Yes," she said and placed her head against his chest, her arms holding him tight for a moment.

"We could do with a preacher here," he said. "Somehow it don't seem fittin' to take a woman with out the words bein' said."

"Love don't come because of the words," Martha said and moved away from him. "We better go on down or the others'll get to thinkin' things."

"Reckon they'd be right," he admitted and picked up the guns. She carried the powder horns and shot bags, following him down the stairs. Her eyes were warm, her mind filled with a woman's thoughts.

The older women had prepared a meal of mush and side meat in Ryker's back quarters. Zelia McClintock's high, complaining voice overrode the others. Ryker's two daughters emerged from the root cellar, wide-eyed and still a little fearful. They were in their early teens, half child, half woman.

Martin and Ryker were still guarding the embrasure

and Emma sat by Martin, her head resting back near his shoulder. Her eyes defied anyone to question her right to be there.

Rain continued to fall in ropy cascades, making the gray day darker and more forlorn. The Comanches under Esqueda still clung to the hill, a dark knot of savagery.

Jubal Caine motioned to his son and Olroyd. They gathered around Brazos.

"What you think, son? Be they dead?"

"I'd say no," Brazos said after a moment's thought. "Old Iron Pants is stubborn enough, but he ain't stupid. I'd say he was holed up along some hillside." He paused to listen to the rain pelt the building. "Them draws and arroyos'll fill up quick."

Mrs. McClintock had come from Ryker's back room in time to hear this verdict of her husband's fate. She was a heavy-faced woman, accustomed to finery and now without it. She did not like the conditions under which she lived and continually searched for someone on whom to lay the blame. Her anger needed an outlet and she chose Martin, who regarded her with a flat, unreadable expression in his eyes.

"You smelly savage," Mrs. McClintock accused. "If you had the courage of a cur dog you'd have stayed with Mr. McClintock instead of runnin' off."

"Now wait a min—" Brazos began, but Martin cut him off.

"Keep out of this! The old hen's talkin' to me." His voice was deep and hard and the enamel brightness of anger was in his eyes. "You want to blame somebody? Then blame Old Iron Pants McClintock! He's th' man who took his bullwhip to Esqueda because a Mexican thought he could eat at the McClintock table. 'Greaser,'

Old Iron Pants called him. 'Get off my land and stay off,' Old Iron Pants told him. His land? Esqueda's forefathers had owned it since Cortez. So Iron Pants got himself a fight to general around. And I get my only brother killed. My own little brother!" Martin's eyes protruded and he trembled. In a more calm voice he said, "To hell with McClintock. Let th' bastard rescue himself!"

McClintock's wife trembled with rage. To her daughter, she shouted, "Get away from him, Emma! Get away, you hear?"

The girl raised her head slowly, looked steadily at her mother, then slipped her arm around Martin's shoulder. Watching, Brazos had to check himself, for the desire to interfere was strong. He thought he understood Emma. She had strong, if so far subdued, yearnings of her own and wanted to break free of her family. Martin was taciturn and in his silences she read a kindred spirit, but Brazos saw a tragedy there.

Martin was not what she needed. He was for no woman; his burning hate pushed aside the possibility of his loving anything except death. Woman amused him—when he was searching for that kind of amusement—and perhaps he would be kind to Emma, for a time. But Martin wanted her mainly because by taking her he would hurt Jeb McClintock.

With this thought in mind, he opened his mouth to speak, but Martha Olroyd put her hand against his chest and stopped him. Zelia McClintock saw that her daughter was defying her before these people and she took a forward step, her fists clenched.

Martha stepped away from Brazos and placed herself between Emma and her mother. "People got a right to make up their own mind," she said. "If there's mistakes to be made, let her make her own."

"Get out of my way before I lay hands on you!"

Placing her fists on her hips, Martha said, "The men won't say anything because you're a woman, but you shut your insultin' mouth or I'll hit you in the face! Now leave Emma alone. She's old enough to decide for herself. If she wants this savage, then let her have him. She'll find out what he's like soon enough."

"Mr. McClintock will have something to say about this!"

"He usually does," Martha said, staring the older woman down. "He's like the wind. He blows so much no one listens to it any more."

Mrs. McClintock gasped and wheeled away. She stood against the far wall, her big arms crossed severely over her breasts, her lined face harsh with anger.

Turning away from the peephole, Ryker said, "Esqueda's holdin' some kind of a pow-wow."

Brazos squinted out and then turned to the others. "He knows McClintock and the others ain't here. When they breast that rise over there, Esqueda'll swoop down like a chicken hawk and cut 'em off, all th' time keepin' out of range of our rifles. Was we to charge him afoot, he'd finish Jeb off and catch us before we could get back inside." Brazos shook his head. "Jeb's not goin' to make it. Never in God's world. Esqueda's spread the trap and Jeb'll put his foot in it."

Mrs. McClintock began to weep and Jubal Caine's wife tried to comfort her. Emma glanced at Martin, then sat with her head tipped forward. Jess Olroyd's face was bleak as he thought about his sons out there. He slapped the maple stock of his Kentucky rifle and said, " We just can't wait here. God damn, my boys—"

"Maybe there's a way," Brazos said and turned to his

father. "Give Martin your Colt's pistol and extra cylinder."

Unbuckling the heavy belt, Caine handed it to the mountain man who still sat against the wall. "What's this for?" Martin asked, his voice deep and unfriendly.

"We're goin' for a walk," Brazos said. "We'll shinny out the back storeroom window and belly up through the grass until we're between Esqueda and the slope Jeb's got to come off of. When he comes in, the Comanches'll ride for him, sure that they got him cut off. Then when they get close enough, we'll break the charge before they know what hit 'em. We'll have th' firepowder, Martin—that's what it'll take."

"Go to hell," Martin said. "We'll both get killed. And what for? That son of a bitch?"

"There's other men out there besides McClintock," Brazos said flatly. "He'll come to our rescue when he sees us."

"He'll damn sure never come to mine. Forget the whole thing."

Brazos left the group of men and stood over Martin, his legs spread, a hard determination on his young face. "Get up, Martin. I won't tell you again."

Martin raised his eyes and locked them with Brazos'. "I'm hurt. You want me to go when I'm hurt?"

"I've seen you hurt worse than that and still fight," Brazos told him. "I mean it, Martin. You and me's givin' Iron Pants a chance."

"Get to your goddamned feet!" Jess Olroyd said softly. He brought the hammer back on his cap-lock rifle and pointed it at Martin's head. "Get up and go with him or I'll blow your brains out; you don't mean a damned thing to me dead or alive."

For a moment it seemed that Martin was going to test

56

Jess Olroyd, then he rolled away from the wall and stood up. He buckled Jubal Caine's Texas pistol on his left hip and lifted his rifle.

"Suppose'n McClintock takes another way in?" Jubal Caine suggested, then shook his head. "Ain't likely though. He's pretty set in his ways."

Brazos indicated that he was ready. He wanted to kiss Martha but felt shy in the presence of the others. No such consideration affected her; she touched him lightly on the cheek and pulled his lips down to hers with this slight pressure. Leaning against him, she spoke to him in that silent way of women, and for a moment Brazos was in favor of letting Esqueda have McClintock and the detachment.

Emma threw her arms around Martin, crying softly.

Her mother's face showed genuine shock and she gave Emma a long, pained look, then hid her face in her hands as Martin grinned and kissed the girl. She moved away from Martin and approached her mother. "I'll be goin' to him tonight. I won't be comin' back, Ma."

"You're lost," Zelia McClintock said. "He'll make a squaw out of you."

"I don't think so, Ma," Emma said.

Martha Olroyd watched this with regret, for she thought that Martin would hurt the girl. The men did not like it either, but they knew Martin; it was worth a man's life to cross him. Only Brazos Caine had ever been able to speak out against Martin and live.

Martha touched Brazos on the arm and her smile beckoned him. "Another kiss for me?"

"You'll be gettin' more than kisses soon," he said boldly.

"Ah," she said softly, "so you think like that, do you?" Her smile deepened. "You'd want many sons."

He went into the back room; Martin followed him with obvious reluctance. Brazos slit the bullhide window with his knife and dropped over the side. Martin looked once at Jess Olroyd, who stood in the doorway, his rifle still handy, then went after Brazos Caine.

CHAPTER SIX

ONCE OUTSIDE, BRAZOS AND MARTIN BELLIED DOWN in the tall grass and began to work their way around to the front of the settlement. Rain was still falling and their buckskins quickly became soaked and clinging. Martin paused to remove his shot pouch and powder horn that served his rifle, placing them beside the sill log of the building. Actually, Martin had no further need of them for when Esqueda and the Comanches charge, they would have time to empty their revolvers and if the charge was not broken, there would be no reloading.

They crawled away from the settlement, their movements slow and cautious. The slanting rain reduced visibility to the point where it was difficult to see the rim where the hostiles waited. Brazos raised himself to all fours and, with pistol in each hand, moved more rapidly. The pressure of the rain bent the tall grass until it was a turbulent brownish-green sea, effectively masking their passage as they slithered through it.

In a half hour they had crawled better than a quarter mile and their knees and elbows were bruised and raw. Martin's side troubled him; his breathing grew ragged at times and pain etched new lines in his face.

Brazos took cautious soundings and when he nodded, Martin moved closer to him. "We're smack-dab in between 'em now," he said softly. "If Iron Pants comes over the ridge, he'll pass about a hundred and fifty yards to the rear of us."

"We could have been on our way to Austin," Martin said between clenched teeth. He shot Brazos a hard glance. "Why th' hell are you wet-nursin' this bunch? You want McClintock's job?"

"You know better'n that," Brazos said. "You're takin' Emma for a wife. You owe the McClintocks somethin', you understand?" He turned his head and looked toward the hills. "Jeb ought to be comin' soon." His eyes lifted to the weeping sky. "I'd judge it to be nine or thereabout. Could be he's takin' it slow and careful."

"If he ain't drowned in some gully," Martin said. "I don't trust that bastard, I sure don't. Be like him to have camped in the hills until daylight, then when he heard the shootin' and whoopin', gone around and come in over the bluff. I'll bet that's it! He's likely ridin' around to come in from the other side of the settlement." Martin pawed at his rain-streaked face. "You got me into this goddamned mess, and if we get out, we got a little set-to comin' up over it."

"If that's the way you want it," Brazos said. "You pick th' time and place."

"I damn sure will," Martin said and pillowed his head in his crossed arms. "Nothin' to do but wait, and I hate waitin'." He seemed unmindful of the discomforting rain.

Nothing stirred except the wind-tossed grass. For an hour they lay there while Brazos raised himself periodically for a reconnoitre. There was no change in Esqueda's position on the hillside although the Indians were showing a marked restlessness.

"You suppose Jeb is really dead?" Brazos asked

worriedly.

Martin swore softly. "My luck's never been that good. Ten years I've been here. Built everythin' up to suit myself, then McClintock's got to come along and start a settlement. I got along with the Indians until he came and spoiled it all with his goddamned laws and high-handed ways.

"Yeah, brother Clay and me had it just the way we wanted it . . . until McClintock whipped Esqueda. Clay, he didn't know it had happened. Just went across the river trappin'. When he didn't come back in a few months I went after him. I found what the buzzards left."

"McClintock didn't kill him," Brazos said.

"He as good as did," Martin said. "Took me a year and some killin' to get the whole story. Clay went to Esqueda's old place and Esqueda turned him loose with likkered up Comanches. Knowin' Comanches, I reckon he died slow and mighty hard." Martin's glance was full of hate. "That's what people do to a land. They can't just live and let it alone, leave it open and free like it's supposed to be. They got to plow it up and sing hymns and let some muckle-head order folks around." Martin ground his teeth together. "He order me around and I'll open up his guts with my knife!"

"People just don't mean nothin' to you," Brazos said. "McClintock's a good man, in spite of his high and mighty ways. If it wasn't for him, a good share of us'd be dead. You don't care about that, do you?"

A gunshot broke through Brazos Cainc's talk and rattled away among the hills. He raised up, as did Martin, and they both began to swear.

From the far slope and five hundred yards below them, McClintock was leading his detachment in Indian

60

file toward the settlement. In some manner they had come over the ridge Brazos and Martin covered, spotted Esqueda and withdrew without being seen. Then, to avoid being cut off, McClintock had gone a couple of miles out of his way and skirted the ridge until he approached the settlement from the bluff's side. Now he had dismounted his troop and was leading them along the steep trail that clung like ladder rungs to the near sheer wall behind Ryker's buildings.

The detail presented a dejected picture, men walking hunch-shouldered, their rifles held against their bodies to protect the weapons from the rain. Traveling off the bluff was slow, cautious work, for a slip meant a fatal plunge to the basin floor. Already, McClintock had led them below the skyline, a dark string of minute moving figures against the sand-colored wall.

"Th' son-of-a-bitchin' smart bastard!" Martin fumed.

Brazos swiveled his head for a look at Esqueda. McClintock's move was smart, for if Esqueda charged now with his warriors, he would have to run the gauntlet of rifles from within the settlement building, a dangerous task.

The Mexican was rallying his Indian followers and Brazos realized what Esqueda planned. By charging now, he would run the risk of the rifles, but he would trap McClintock and party on the bluffs, without cover.

Then another, more ominous thought came to Brazos Caine. When Esqueda charged off the slope, he would effectively cut off Brazos and Martin from the settlement. McClintock's new strategy had been good for it altered the odds and the lines of battle, but in increasing his own chances of survival, Jeb McClintock had reduced Brazos' and Martin's to zero.

Brazos surveyed the situation with detached calm. He

61

realized that running for the settlement now was their only chance. It wasn't much of a chance; the odds against their making it were too great. Possibly they might narrow the gap and gain McClintock's support . . .

"We'll have to run for it," Brazos said, jumping to his feet, a Colt's pistol in each hand.

"We ain't goin' to make it," Martin said tightly but came erect when Brazos did. A loud whooping began behind them as the Comanches saw them and from that moment on it was a grim race. The pain in Martin's side slowed him and Brazos held back to stay with him.

After covering seventy yards at a dead run, Brazos shouted, "This is as far as we go," and whirled; the Comanche ponies were close now. An arrow sped past him and buried itself in the grass. Along the line of approaching horsemen, balls of smoke whipped up and away as muskets were discharged.

The air was full of ringing whoops and Brazos knelt beside Martin, their long-barreled pistols cracking, recoiling, then cracking again. Three ponies trotted away riderless while bowstrings twanged and arrows thudded into the ground.

Now and then a trade musket rattled and the ball sang past, but Brazos and Martin fired with cool care. The hostiles were no more than twenty yards away. With the charges in the Comanche muskets exhausted, they reverted to the battle lance; others wheeled their horses in jumping circles as they tried to reload. The two men sighted on these warriors and brought three more down before the charge split and they galloped away to each side of them.

Behind them, McClintock and his men hurried down the slope and Olroyd, Ryker and the others within the building ran out and charged up the hill toward Brazos and Martin. Then, kneeling like fusiliers, they fired a volley at a range of one hundred yards and ponies went down or were wiped clean of their riders. Esqueda launched another wave. The line of kneeling men at the bottom of the hill wavered as this charge swept toward them, but McClintock, who was near the bottom now, ordered his men to fire at the attackers.

Ryker fell back, his rifle forgotten as he clutched his thigh. Jess Olroyd cried out, slapped a hand to his breast and fell forward on his face. Around Brazos and Martin a furious battle raged. They fired their pistols at pointblank range; Brazos fell flat on his stomach to break the cylinder pin and slip his fresh cylinder in place. A moment later he was firing again.

Esqueda and his Mexican followers had moved closer and one raised a battered bugle to his lips and blew a series of sharp tones. Martin's one pistol had been emptied and discarded, as had been his rifle. Now he aimed Jubal Caine's Texas pistol, shot at a wheeling brave who leveled a musket at him, and missed.

The brave shot, and Brazos was flung back by the ball; he lay face down, his breathing pinched. His eyes refused to focus and it required all his effort to raise himself on an elbow and cock his pistol. The Comanche had discarded his empty musket and was poising his lance for the kill. Brazos sighted as well as he could and felt it recoil. When the smoke cleared, the Comanche was on the ground, his face a red smear.

The screaming Indians were re-forming for another sweep. The piercing notes of the bugle rallied them, but they never formed. A new set of rifles added their voice to the din of battle as McClintock raced to the front of the settlement. Men formed into the prone, kneeling and standing position and fired by volley on command.

Only a dozen or so braves remained in the battle. Esqueda and his handful of Mexicans were relatively unscathed, for the Comanches had taken the brunt of the Texan's fire. Now he gathered his men for the rush and threw out a ragged battle line. There was only the slap of pistol and rifle fire from the settlement to bother him now.

Esqueda had seen the effect Martin and Brazos had achieved with their repeating pistols and understood that they would have to be eliminated before he could successfully sweep on to complete victory. This was the moment of attack for Esqueda, when the firepower was on his side. McClintock's men were frantically reloading and the Colts of Brazos and Martin were nearly empty.

Waving a silver-mounted Texas pistol in each hand, Esqueda drove his white horse with knee commands and led the charge toward the two men in the grass. Muskets popped and then Brazos lifted himself and squared Esqueda briefly in the sights before squeezing the trigger. The Colt roared and belched a wad of smoke. When this drifted away, Esqueda was reeling in the saddle. He had dropped his silver-mounted guns and was clutching the saddlehorn with both hands as he dug in his spurs.

Martin turned his pistol on the Mexican and shot until his charges were exhausted. The great white horse faltered in mid-stride, then bent at the foreleg, cascading Esqueda to the ground.

Again the bugler blew frantically and the Mexicans rallied around the fallen man. The Comanches continued to yell, but the charge had been broken. With one remaining load in his gun, Brazos raised his revolver, downing the man who tried to lift Esqueda to another horse. Martin cursed his empty guns. They watched the Mexicans bear Esqueda away.

A moment later the attackers faded from sight beyond the brow of a hill. Martin, by good fortune, had escaped further injury. McClintock's men were running through the rain toward them and Martin helped Brazos to his feet.

The aftermath of the fight was working on everyone's nerves and they all talked at once in a senseless babble. When Jubal Caine put an arm around his son to support him, Martin walked over to the spot where he had shot Esqueda and retrieved the Mexican's guns. The men turned downhill and were walking back to the settlement; Martin, who did not fit in, walked twenty yards behind them.

Martha Olroyd insisted that Brazos be taken upstairs and placed in bed. Ryker wanted to cut the bullet out in the barroom, but Martha was adamant. Her brothers carried Jess Olroyd inside and laid him on the floor. She glanced at him and felt the tears well up in her eyes, but she dashed them away.

Someone noticed that Ryker had taken a musket ball through the thigh muscle, but he would let no one touch it. He poured a cup of corn whiskey over it, howled and jumped up and down a few times and pronounced it cured.

Mrs. Olroyd leaned against the wall, a deadness in her eyes, her lips moving soundlessly. She was remembering other times when her flesh and blood had lain on the floor as her husband now lay. Jubal Caine raised his head and looked at Martha and found her eyes wet, but she was not openly crying.

Martin had helped Brazos up the stairs and into a room. Martha followed with a bucket of hot water and cloth from Ryker's shelves. After stripping off his buckskin shirt, she examined the wound. Finally she said, "We'll have to do some cuttin', Brazos." Her hide slippers shuffled on the rough plank floor.

"Let me have a look there," Martin said. He probed the wound with a dirty finger until Brazos knocked his hand away. "Yep," Martin said. "Th' ball's still in there." He smiled and his lips pulled away from his teeth. "Want me to belt you one or are you tough like an Apache?"

Sweat was a-shine on Brazos' face and his hair was rain-plastered against his forehead. "I'll take it," he said, glaring at Martin.

Laughing softly, Martin took out his Green River knife and struck steel against flint to ignite a candle. He passed the steel through the flames a couple of times, then sat on the edge of the bed.

Martha watched this with increasing alarm, then she struck out and knocked the knife from Martin's hand. "What do you think you're going to do?" she asked.

Martin looked at her innocently. "Only tryin' to help him."

"Or see if you can make him yell!" she snapped. "Get out!"

"Hell, I—" Martin stood up, uncertain with this fury facing him.

"Get the hell out!" Martha flared. "Is that plain enough for you to understand?" She hit him in the chest with the flat of her hand, driving him a step toward the door. "He's my man. I'll take care of him, you understand?"

"Hell, yes," Martin said and went out, slamming the door behind him. Martha went downstairs and came back a few minutes later with a small, thin-bladed knife

66

and ran it through the candle flame. Her hands were shaking and she pressed them against her stomach until the trembling stopped. Suddenly she hated Martin with an almost overwhelming fury. The man had intended to carve Brazos with that knife!

She had seen the work of rough frontier surgery, a mass of angry scars to mark a man the rest of his life. Brazos watched her and tried to understand her anger. Then he said, "I could use a Kentucky breakfast about now."

"What's that?"

"A bottle of blue ruin, a steak and a dog."

"What's the dog for?" she asked, puzzled.

"To eat the steak," Brazos said. He fumbled for his pistol belt and folded it before clamping his teeth on it. She looked at him, pain and an apology in her eyes for the hurt she was about to cause him. Then she took a deep breath and leaned over him.

He arched his back when the knife went in. Sweat dripped from his face. He made no outcry other than a gargling moan deep in his chest. She had to turn the knife to probe for the ball and his eyes glazed and the corded neck muscles stood out like ropes beneath his skin.

Then she had it out, slightly mashed where it had struck bone. Perspiration ran down her checks and soaked her thin dress across the back and under the arms. She gripped the edge of the bed and trembled, and when this stopped, took the leather belt from between his teeth.

"Now—the powder," he said and she uncapped his flask.

In the open wound she poured a small amount, then picked up the candle. With the sudden hiss of the powder igniting, he cried out and then fainted. The room was thick with smoke; it hovered in a cloud among the ceiling beams.

While he was still she bandaged the shoulder, putting plenty of bear grease around the wound to minimize the scabbing. The door opened and Brazos' mother came in, a short woman with a plump face. She looked at her son with a mother's worry.

"He'll be fine," Martha said.

"He's my last," she said softly. She touched the girl and smiled. "I can see how it is with you two. Why don't you stay th' nights with us an' take care of him durin' the day? His cabin's close by."

"All right," Martha said and watched the older woman go out.

Brazos opened his eyes and lay staring at the ceiling. His shoulder was a bundle of pain and it throbbed with every heartbeat. Across the river tonight, another man would be writhing on his soft bed while his *mozo* probed for a bullet. He wondered where he had hit the Mexican and whether or not it had been fatal.

Martin came in again and laid Esqueda's silver-mounted Colt on the rough quilt. He gave Martha a nervous glance and the girl returned it, unfriendly, untrusting. "These are yours," Martin said.

"See that Jeb McClintock gets my other pistols then," Brazos said.

Martin seemed insulted. "Iron Pants? By Jesus, I'd rather see some damned Apache have 'em!"

"I bought 'em," Brazos said, "and they're mine. And I say he can have 'em."

"Then give 'em to him yourself," Martin said tightly and slammed out of the room. Martha turned her head and studied the closed door.

"He hates so bitterly," she said. She sat on the edge of his bed, her hands touching the silver-mounted guns. A silversmith across the river had applied his art in beautiful patterns; the handles had been carved out of horn, then polished.

She held up one of the pistols. "Was it worth it, Brazos?"

"What?"

"This. That's all you got to show for the bullet. Was it worth it?"

He shook his head from side to side, not having an answer for her. He had won, but he had nothing tangible to point to, only the feeling that he had taken an important step. He only half understood his own ambitions, but he dreamed of great things. One day there would be roads and he would own wagons to travel those roads. Perhaps even a store like Vrain and Gooding's at Fort Davis. He didn't know exactly, but he felt that he had been placed here to await the opportunity that was to come.

He was very tired now. Martha bent over him and pressed her lips against his, then lay down beside him and pulled a rough blanket over them. She slid her arm beneath his head and lay looking at his face. From within him he felt an answering stir at her nearness.

He touched the curve of her hip with a caressing gesture. Beneath her thin dress she wore nothing and her skin was warm and soft through the cloth. Because he loved her he was keenly conscious of her poverty, the poverty that touched them all, save himself, for he sold his furs for gold. He decided that he would get her some cloth at Fort Davis. Perhaps a new dress and the soft things to be worn beneath it.

Softly, she said, "Can't you wait?" His hand stopped

caressing her. "We'll talk about marryin' when you're well."

"Waitin's for fools and old people," he said and kissed her demandingly. But she drew back and pushed him away. He sighed contentedly and lay back again, his eyes closed. Before he fell asleep he could hear her regular breathing beside him.

CHAPTER SEVEN

MARTIN RESTED AGAINST THE WALL, A GREAT weariness pushing at him. His throbbing wound and a night without sleep were a weight on his shoulders, and strain made deep lines in his face.

But he could not relax for he was without friends here; their attitude toward him was clear. McClintock's son, Forney, was in Ryker's back room having a bandage put on his arm where a musket ball had grazed it. Sykes had a broken leg and was moaning softly on a pallet in the far corner.

Jeb McClintock sat on the counter, his legs dangling over the edge. Near his hand was the brace of Colt's Texas pistols that Brazos Caine had given him. Olroyd was stretched out on the bar, a blanket thrown over him; Mrs. Olroyd sat silent and staring into space. Olroyd's sons were hunkered down by the wall on the store side.

These people were without tears or regret for life was too primitive, too elemental for the luxury of remorse. A man was born, lived for a time, then died; they had learned that nothing could change the pattern. Acceptance of death came easy.

McClintock touched the pistols and said softly, "Makes a man ashamed, indeed it does. Could be I've

70

misjudged the boy." He let out a sigh and added, "I hate to think our number has been reduced by tragedy, but on the whole, the expedition was a success. Esqueda's been hurt and his band shot up considerable. We should have done this long ago—I've always said it."

Martin raised his head and stared at the men. "You goddamned fool! You think it's over?" He laughed hollowly and fell silent.

McClintock's wrinkled face grew severe. "Martin you have no voice with me. You've spoken against me and I take that from no man, even you." He came off the counter and stood before Martin. "You're hurt and I want no advantage. When you're well, I'll meet you with pistols."

"That makes me right pleased," Martin said, his eyes flat and expressionless.

"Nobody's goin' to meet anybody," Jubal Caine said. "There's been enough dyin' around here as it is."

Swiveling his head around, McClintock stared at Caine. "I've a score to settle with this man when he can stand."

"Do that and I'll put a ball through you," Caine said. "Back down once, Jeb. You've made a passel of mistakes, bad ones. I'd say we'd best forget 'em, you and everybody else."

"I have my duty as I see it," McClintock stated. "My orders can't be flouted and still preserve discipline." He looked again at the Texas pistols that Brazos had given him. "I see through your son's scheme. He put me in a bad light by guessing Esqueda's intent. Now he has given me these pistols to show the people that Jeb McClintock can be bought." He held up the guns. "Thirty dollars apiece in New Orleans, and yet he gives them away as though they were worthless. I've seen

71

these kind of men before. They grow rich while hard-working men want." He speared Martin with his eyes. "What has this man given to the settlement? I ask you now to tell—"

"You shut up!" Martin got to his feet. His face was dark with anger and his hand brushed the butt of his pistol. "You son of a bitch, I've heard enough from you!"

"I've had enough of both of you!" Jubal Caine said. Martin and McClintock shot him glances and froze. Caine had his pistol pointed between them. He said, "Martin, you just take your paws away from that Colt and sit back down."

"No man puts a pistol on me," Martin said.

"I'm puttin' one on you," Jubal said. "Now mind me proper before you get hurt permanent-like."

Martin resumed his place, his hand pressing against his injured side. McClintock stood rooted, his face working uncontrollably.

"I've been thinkin'," Caine said, "and it seems to me that we're hangin' on by our thumbs here. I'm sick to the belly of it. My boy's been hankerin' to get into the tradin' business and I think his idea's sound. He tells me that there's movers around Fort Davis and San Felipe de Austin. That right, Martin?"

"There's people there," Martin admitted grudgingly. "There's too many people here now, stinkin' up the country. What do you want more for? More like him?" He nodded to McClintock.

"We ain't growin'," Jubal insisted. "With new folks, we would."

McClintock looked around the room at the faces before speaking. "I'm in authority here and I haven't considered this plan as yet."

"You don't have to," Anse Moreclay said. He sat

72

against the wall, his feet tucked beneath him. "You had your chance, Jeb, and fell down as far as I'm concerned. If it hadn't been for young Caine, the lot of us would have been dead." He glanced at Martin and added, "Brazos said you and him was goin' to Austin. How long before you can travel?"

"Ten days. Possibly two weeks."

"What you gettin' at, Anse?" Sykes asked. He stopped his moaning and was propped up on an elbow, interested.

"I done my turn in the militia in 1812," Moreclay stated, "and what we need is solid fortification here instead of just rifles."

"I'll send through an official request," McClintock began, but Moreclay cut him off with the wave of a hand.

"Official be damned! You couldn't get a message out if you wanted to. You think the militia cares what happens to us out here? They've forgot we're alive. Now there's cannon at Fort Davis. That's what we need, three or four stout five-pounders on the second floor to fire across the valley. No Injun would come within two miles of the place after bein' shot at a couple of times."

"I'll need time to think this out," McClintock said. "Men, as your leader—"

"Leader, your ass," Ray Olroyd said flatly. "We followed you all night on a damned goose-chase. That's my pa in there on the bar, Jeb. What you got to say about that?"

"I—I'm sorry," McClintock offered lamely. "Both sides lose men in battle, Ray."

"Your side always loses," Olroyd said. "I'm sick of you, McClintock. I've had enough. Let's put it to a vote, men. Those in favor of Brazos Caine takin' Jeb

73

McClintock's place, raise your hand."

He looked around the room and counted slowly. Sykes had his hand up, as did Ryker. Moreclay hesitated a moment, then raised his, and his sons followed. Povy remained stoutly for McClintock, as did McClintock's sons. But Jubal Caine raised his hand, and with the Olroyd's, out-voted the McClintock faction.

Nodding, McClintock spoke stiffly. "Very well. I can see that my judgment no longer has weight. I'll concede defeat to Brazos Caine, but this is not ended, not by a jugful." He stepped to the door and paused there. Emma stood near Martin and this aroused McClintock's anger still further. "Keep away from my girl. That's a flat warnin'!" He spoke to Martin, then flicked his eyes to Emma. "Get along home now."

"We're goin' to marry," Emma said. "Ain't that so, Martin?"

"Yeah," Martin said softly. "You all heard it. I'm takin' me a wife."

"By Jesus, no, I said!" McClintock came back into the room, his legs stiff. Martin rolled away from the wall and came up with his knife.

"Come on," he invited. "I always wanted to open your guts!"

"Reckon you both better ease off," Jubal Caine drawled. His pistol was out again and cocked as he covered McClintock. "Simmer down, Jeb. The girl's made up her mind. Leave it lay now."

"I forbid such an alliance!" McClintock spoke through tight jaws.

"Take her and git!" said Jubal. Martin moved toward the door with Emma. "I ain't doin' this because I like you, Martin, but because she deserves better'n she's got. Now you treat her good or I'll come after your ears."

"You makin' a threat to me?" Martin asked.

"A promise," Jubal said. "You got the others buffaloed, but me you ain't. I've curried tougher hounds than you'll ever be and I'm still here. My boy'll be up to see you when he's fit to travel. You be ready."

"I'll be ready," Martin said and went out with Emma.

Martin closed the door behind him and they left the settlement. The rain was a steady drizzle and a deep grayness painted the hills with a dark veil. Martin moved ahead of her, breaking down the wet grass as he moved away from Ryker's. His side pained him fiercely and he walked slowly. A half hour later they paused on the first ridge to look back. Ryker's was small and forlorn-looking against the grim backdrop of the high bluff.

"We'll make it home by nightfall," he said and turned with her, leading the way along the ridge. The natural caution never left Martin and he cradled his Colt's rifle across his chest as he moved along. His pistol banged against his leg and hip as he dodged niggerheads and clumps of dripping brush.

In the late afternoon he dipped into the brush-choked hollow where he left his parfleche and sat down to rest. The rain had reduced Emma's hair to straggles and her homespun dress was soaked through, clinging to her body in heavy folds.

Emma carried the parfleche when they worked their way out of the hollow. After a while she said, "I'm bringin' you nothin' and it makes me ashamed." She pulled at the rough material clinging to her breasts and slogging around her legs. "One dress and bullhide slippers, about eat through."

He did not break his stride, but turned his head to speak. "Who cares about a woman's dress?"

She stared at him, for the intensity of his voice shocked her. "You, you won't—hurt me, will you, Martin?"

He laughed. "How can you hurt a woman?"

Darkness began to fall early and the rain slackened off to a heavy mist when Martin led down into the valley where his cabin stood at a lonely distance. The sight of it stirred him to an increased pace and he came off the down-tilting slope with Emma half-running to keep up.

He entered the yard, his head swinging from side to side. "Follow me close," he said. "The yard is full of traps."

Opening the door of his cabin, he took the parfleche from her and tossed it in the corner. He struck steel and flint for a light. The punk sputtered with a bluish glow, then the candle flickered and a sickly light spread over the table, leaving the corners and walls in semi darkness.

"Get a fire going," he said and stripped off his buckskin shirt. He barred the door next. The cabin was small with cured buffalo hide covering the window openings. Near the top of the walls, slits opened up to the outside and a narrow catwalk gave a man enough room to crawl from one firing position to another.

Martin hung his buckskin near the fireplace. His bare upper body gleamed damply and he removed the bloody bandage. Taking tobacco, he crushed it between his palms and rebandaged his side. The tobacco would draw out the soreness. From his parfleche he took a blanket and handed it to Emma. "Get your dress dry," he said.

"I'm all right," she said and huddled near the blaze.

"Do I have to rip it off?"

The mildness of his voice shocked her more than if he

76

had shouted. There was a polish to his eyes as he watched her, and she untied the rawhide string running down her back. She let the dress fall and stood with the rich light playing on her smooth skin. She wouldn't look at him, but stared at her bare feet. Martin laughed softly and she slipped the blanket around her, covering her nakedness.

"I'll fix you somethin' to eat," she offered lamely.

"It can wait," he said and watched her until color climbed into her face. He crossed suddenly to the mantel for his pipe, and she shrank back a step before she realized that he had not intended to touch her. He went to the candle for his light. "You afraid of me, Emma?"

"I don't know," she whispered.

The darkness deepened to ink outside and some of it crept into the small room, blackening the shadows along the rough walls, making the dancing flames in the fireplace seem brighter. His shirt began to steam and he turned it. She did not move this time when he passed near her, and he reached out and touched her while she fought down a rising panic.

"You've led me along," Martin said. "I get tired of that."

There was no sound in the room except the pop of the fire and Martin's heavy breathing. She stood like an ivory figure and he raised her chin before pulling her against him. His kiss was rough and full of desire and the blanket fell away while his hands moved over her body. Only then did she seem to become conscious of his intent, and she pushed against his chest.

"No!" she cried. "Martin, no!"

"I took you for a wife," he said, his lips seeking hers again. "Now goddammit, act like one!"

She writhed free. "I'm afraid! Of you, this place!" She began to cry and tears made bright streaks down her cheeks. Her voice was breathless and the words came in a rush. "I—I want to go back home, Martin. Take me back, please take me back."

"Take you back, hell," he said. "You want to make a fool of me in front of the settlement? Is that what you want?"

When she reached for the blanket he swept it into the corner with his foot. "You won't be needin' that," he said and grabbed her arm.

Emma whirled, tried to break away, but he fisted her hair and pulled her back. Her hands pushed at him, shoving him and he laughed at her struggles.

Raising her legs, she tried to shove him back and he struck her across the mouth. "Goddammit, now lay still!"

Blood welled from her cut lip. The room was suddenly unbearably hot and stuffy. Emma closed her eyes tightly and went limp. Her crying was hushed.

Finally he left her and went to the mantel to get his pipe. She heard his bare feet padding on the dirt floor, but didn't open her eyes to look at him.

He stood with his back to the flames, a blocky silhouette, the smoke from his pipe gray wreaths around his face. He studied her, the burning flags of his hunger diminished in his eyes.

Finally he said, "You're worse than an Apache squaw. You wouldn't have hollered if I'd killed you."

"I want to go home," Emma said softly.

"You're stayin'," Martin said softly. "Run and I'll strip some hide off your back. You know what you have to do. See that you do it."

He threw his sleeping robe over her and blew out the

candle, then lay down beside her. For a long while he lay there and listened to her breathing. A deep silence descended over the cabin and the night melted slowly into dawn.

CHAPTER EIGHT

BRAZOS CAINE COULD RECALL THE TIME WHEN nineteen families had lived around Ryker's settlement, but violence and discouragement had reduced the ranks to ten, counting Martin.

The morning following the attack, Brazos walked slowly the quarter mile from Ryker's to his own cabin. Martha was with him and he opened the door for her. In spite of his wild mountain ways, Brazos Caine was a builder; the improvements on his cabin showed this. Because he trapped, he had gold to spend and his kitchen boasted the only complete set of iron pans and skillets in the settlement.

His place had two rooms, three if you counted the shed attached to the rear. There were four windows and a front and back door, and one section of the interior was partitioned off with hanging buffalo hides. These could be drawn together, separating completely his sleeping quarters from the rest of the cabin.

The stone fireplace was large and drew well; the hearth was laid with careful smoothness and there were shaved planks covering the floor. Martha smiled when she saw this and took off her rawhide slippers to walk back and forth, her feet whispering on the bare surface. "My," she said delightedly. "I've always dreamed of a floor beneath my feet." She shot him a laughing glance. "You'll never keep shoes on me now."

A short ladder led into the loft and she climbed it for a brief inspection. Here was his fur cache, mounds of pelts stacked to the roof. She came back down and said, "I expect you have a thousand dollars worth there, Brazos."

"Wouldn't be surprised," he said. "Now you can see why I've got to get my carts through."

Along one wall Brazos had built cupboards for his provisions and near the top, a rack held a row of china plates with saucers hanging from hooks. Martha touched the planed wood and she knew how patiently he must have worked with drawknife and bit to have fitted these so closely. In the entire building there was not a nail; everything was held together with ash pegs. The furniture was handmade, but he had four chairs, a large table and his stout bed. Several bear hides served as rugs.

She went behind the buffalo-hide curtain and he heard the shucks rustle as she tested the bed. When she came back he was sitting by the table, his arm bound tightly to his chest. He said, "Do you like it?"

"Yes," she said softly and sat down across from him, her bare arms crossed. "Yes, I like it, but it's not what I expected." Her eyes left his face, wandered about the room and came back. He possessed the little things, dishes, candlesticks, all the items dear to a woman. "I didn't know you had this, Brazos. You're not like the others. You dream, and I like that." She rubbed her hand over the table top. "What made you build like this?"

"A woman," he said frankly and smiled. "Not just any woman, but one woman."

"Me?"

He shrugged. "As it turned out—yes." He laughed self-consciously. "But I wasn't thinkin' of anyone

80

special. I lived in a soddy and it wasn't enough. A man can't keep goin' with nothin' in his head, Martha. He gets tired of walkin' when there's no place to go." Brazos left his chair and opened the door so he could see the inscrutable distance. He stood there, watching this gray day and Martha came to his side, putting her arm lightly about him.

"What do you see out there that I don't see?" she asked. When he glanced quickly at her, she added, "I know you see something different. I've watched you before when you looked like that."

His shoulders rose and fell slightly. "A road," he said and drew her sharpened attention. "A good road with my wagons travelin' on it; that's what I see. Wagons with my name on the sides and piled high with goods for my tradin' post." He raised his good arm and made a sweep toward the mountains. "I'm not much for plantin' cotton and rakin' a bean patch. There's plews out there, and buff'lo yonder. Hides, not beans, is the thing, Martha. I trade 'em for what I want and the rest goes into my account at Vrain and Gooding's tradin' post. I got nineteen hundred dollars in gold there." He said this proudly as though he alone had discovered a reason for living in this alien land.

"I guess you're rich then," Martha said. "Nineteen hundred dollars is a heap of money."

"Money's a tool," Brazos said. "Like an ax. Martin and me's goin' to Fort Davis in a few days. I'll take a load or two out and bring some back. That'll be the beginnin'." He glanced down at her and smiled. "I'll bring you some pretties so you can look good for the marryin'. A woman ought to have somethin' special then."

"I don't need anything but what I have," she said

81

seriously.

His smile deepened, crinkling the skin of his face. "Every woman needs more than she has," he said and turned back inside.

She fixed a meal for him and he watched her move around the cabin, the sway of her hips holding his interest. He sat down by the table while she worked. He did not speak while she set the table, and while they ate he remained silent. But after pushing his empty plate aside, he said, "I'm real pleased with you, Martha."

"No more than pleased?" The shadow of a smile lurked along the ends of her lips. She was more than pretty and knew it and she brought him out of his chair and around the table. He encircled the small circumference of her waist with his good arm and swept her against him. She laughed and then kissed him. When she turned away, her face was flushed with a new excitement. He would have kissed her again but voices came softly to him across the clearing and he moved to the door.

Jeb McClintock and his oldest son were walking across the yard and Brazos waved. Martha came to the door to see who it was and then turned back to the fire and filled the blackened coffeepot, hanging it on the crane.

"We just ate or I'd invite you in for a bite," Brazos said as McClintock came in with his son. Asa squatted against the wall while the old man settled himself at the table. Asa watched Martha with a brooding intensity until he became aware of Brazos' blunt stare, then he tipped his head forward and studied his hands.

"You've got it tolerable here," McClintock said slowly. "Never had the occasion to come here before, but I always wondered what you were buildin'. Seems that every time I looked this way a hammer or saw was goin'." He shifted in the chair and crossed his long legs. "I'd build my own place bigger, but Esqueda takes delight in bedevilin' me. Seems such a waste, all that work just to make a fire for him and his heathen followers."

"Move in closer to the settlement," Brazos suggested. "Then a neighbor could watch your place while you was away."

"Like it where I'm at," the old man said. "A mile's close enough for one man to live next to another." He turned his head softly. "By Jesus, is that coffee I smell?" He rubbed his bony hands together. "Been out of coffee for more'n five months."

Martha set the pot and three cups on the table. McClintock turned one over in his hands. "Fine dishes," he said and pursed his lips. "Likely you got a tidy sum put away to afford knickknacks like these." He poured and passed the pot to his son. "But that's neither here nor there. Since I've been voted out of my rightful authority, I came over to offer any help I can. I guess you want to make some changes."

"I'm goin' to do away with the tithings," Brazos said. "The grain and victuals I'll have divided up and give back."

McClintock's eyes opened wide. "Man, you can't do that! What'll some do for food?"

"Starve," Brazos said and sipped his coffee. "Jeb, I guess you been takin' *too* good care of these folks and some is downright lazy because of it. Bushrod Povy's been eatin' off th' others for two years now. Why should he break his back workin' when he knows you'll never let him and his woman starve?" Brazos shook his head. "The way I see it, the tithin's folks have turned

83

into Ryker's storehouse is the profit on their crops. Grain, cured meat, dried greens, hides—all belong to the people who gathered 'em. Jeb, men like Povy are leeches and as long as someone'll work for 'em, they won't turn a lick. He'll either shift for himself now or get out; I don't care which."

McClintock was surprised and somewhat worried. "A grave step," he said. "We're a common lot and we must stick together. What is one man's misfortune is misfortune to all."

"No," Brazos said forcefully. "Jeb, we're landlocked and I mean to change that. Martin and me's goin' to open a road through to Fort Davis and maybe San Felipe de Austin. I'm goin' into the tradin' business, Jeb. I'll buy grain, meat, hides, bone—anythin' you can catch or raise. Buy it here for gold or credits in trade at my store. And I'll run all the risks of gettin' my stuff through."

"By grab!" McClintock exclaimed. "Mighty big ambition."

"I got ten Mexican wagons now," Brazos said and refilled his coffee cup. "When I come back I'll have 'em loaded." He smiled at McClintock's amazement. "Pass the word around that I'm payin' a dollar and a half a day, gold on the barrel head, for men. I aim to have my place up before I leave."

"Sufferin' Moses," Asa said softly. "I never heard of wages like that."

"You'll earn 'em if you work for me," Brazos assured him.

Jeb McClintock said, "Was my back in shape, I'd take some of that myself." He got up and motioned his son to his feet. "I'll see that word gets around, Caine. Damn, man, if you and that savage can get through regular enough we'll be gettin' new families in here."

84

With a brief nod to Martha, McClintock started off across the shallow valley, his son at his heels.

Brazos and Martha stood for a time in the open doorway watching him. When they were near Ryker's buildings, she said, "Can you get through with a train of carts?"

"Not unless I try," he told her. "Be no trouble with th' Comanches 'cause we're too far from th' river and that's Apache country."

"There hasn't been a wagon in here for a year," she said and gave him a worried glance before turning inside.

At daybreak the next morning, Brazos Caine found a dozen men at his door. He gave his orders and watched them move toward the timber two miles away. When they returned with the first logs, he had marked out the site for his store, and in spite of one arm being in a sling, had managed to drive the corner stakes.

All during the day the ring of ax and the sloughing of adz lay over the valley. The weather was cloudy but here was no rain. By nightfall the base logs were sunk and notched and most of the floor joists were in place.

For two days the laboring continued, dawn to dark, and on the afternoon of the third day, a drizzling rain began, but no one quit. Brazos Caine paid wages in gold every night, the first money that had been seen in the settlement for over a year. And because they wanted to see more of it, the store went up with great speed.

Ryker came over on the fourth day and stood with his hands on his hips while men fitted rafters and peaked the roof. He stood near Brazos and said, "I'll ask you again—come in with me."

"I want a place of my own," Brazos said and Ryker snorted.

"Not enough business here for two stores and you know it."

"I know it," Brazos said. "So I'm going to take yours."

Ryker sighed and tried again. "I got a shed full of goods. You get that through and there'll be profit in it for both of us." He slapped his hands together and looked exasperated. "You're tryin' to squeeze me out, is that it?"

"No," Brazos said. "Ryker, you've squeezed yourself out. You've been tryin' to run a business without a supply line and it won't work. Your shelves are damned near empty and your hide house is stuffed. You need trade goods and can't get it. Now I got money and I might have the supply line. When I get my own place stocked I'll talk to you about movin' your stuff to Fort Davis."

"You *do* mean to run me out!" Ryker snapped.

"Go haul it yourself then."

"You got all the wagons!"

"Haul 'em from across the river like I did," Brazos said.

Ryker moaned softly and watched three men split shakes for the roof. "Dammit, I can't get through to Fort Davis and you know it!"

"Why not? Don't you know th' way?"

"To hell with you!" Ryker snapped. "You think I'll get killed for a goddamned dollar?"

"That's for you to decide," Brazos said and watched Ryker stalk back to his settlement house.

On the eighth day the store was completed and Brazos sent Antrim McClintock around to all the cabins, inviting the people in for a housewarming party. A quarter of a mile away, his father's cabin nestled against the brow of a cone-shaped hill. Smoke rose sluggishly from the stick and mud chimney, then was swirled away by the erratic wind. From the grayness of the day, Brazos judged there would be more rain and turned inside his cabin to help Martha.

He no longer wore his sling, but the shoulder was stiff and when he moved it, he did so gingerly. Opening a trap door in the floor, he let himself down into the hole. Martha handed him a candle and he disappeared completely for several minutes. Finally he came up with three jugs which he placed on the edge of the doorway. "Sorghum molasses, the only molasses between here and Fort Davis. Cost me three prime pelts and I had to fight the fella for it."

The second trip produced three large hams and four slabs of bacon. He kicked the trap door shut and toed a bear rug over it. "Was folks to know I had that," he said, "they'd be eatin' here twice a week." He went outside and sat on the chopping block while Martha started the big meal.

Toward evening they began to gather, the McClintocks, the Olroyds, Povy, Moreclay—across the valley they came. The women went inside to help Martha carry the kettles and pots of food into the store.

The men stood around admiring the building. At least fifty feet square, it was built like a blockhouse. Rope and pulleys were fastened on each upper corner to hoist the cannon to the breastwork. The loopholes were high on the upper tier, the slits much too high to be reached from the ground.

There were no windows at all on the ground floor. Around the top of the eaves, openings let in light and air, but a raiding party would need a ladder to get in.

Jubal Caine produced a gallon jug. "Been savin'

this," he said and passed it around. They drank mountain-style, their finger hooked in the handle, the jug supported by a bent elbow.

Sykes pointed to the embrasures. He leaned heavily on crutches, his left leg splinted. "You figure on puttin' cannon up there?"

"If I can get 'em," Brazos said. He listened to the soft run of women's talk coming from the building. "I guess the eatin' is about to commence," he said and led the way.

The long counter was the table and everyone ate standing. Martha had baked the cornbread and with the sorghum molasses and meat, everyone ate their fill. The men ate at one end while the women talked near the back of the room. Ray Olroyd produced a jug and set this on the counter with the exactitude of the three-quarters drunk.

As the meal drew to an end, Olroyd's drunkenness grew pronounced and he became talkative. He tried to start an argument with several men, but they pushed him away. Finally he got to Brazos Caine.

"Well," he said and grinned oafishly, "our hero. I've been thinkin' about you—I sure have. I'll bet Asa over there is thinkin' about you right now." Ray sniggered. "Asa's put out at you, Brazos. He don't like to see Martha here. You know what he's wonderin' right now?"

"Shut your drunken mouth," Brazos said and a hush came over the men. Ray's brothers, Jethro and Clem, too sat motionless against the wall. The men stood around, listening.

Some of the laughter froze on Ray Olroyd's face and he weaved uncertainly on his feet. "Hell," he said thickly, "I was only tellin' the truth. You don't want to hear the truth, s'all right with me. But ripe fruit's for the pickin'."

"*I said shut up!*"

"Suresuresuresuresure," Ray mumbled. He took his jug from the counter and staggered over to the wall. He sat down heavily, still mumbling to himself, then his head drooped forward. With his long arms hooked around his jug he sat in a bent-over position, staring at nothing. Finally he keeled over and lay in a heap, the jug nestled in the crook of his arm.

From the end of the room, Mrs. Olroyd looked at her son. "Drunken lot I married into," she said. "Just like his father was." Her voice was darkly mournful. "All the good boys died. There was Gamaliel and Caleb together. Abram was next, then Jesse and Alvina. Belinda and Dinah, I never knew about them. The beasties got 'em when I was washin' and I never seen 'em again."

The women looked at each other and the men frowned. Martha felt that she should defend her mother, although she sometimes wished that her mother wouldn't talk this way. Martha said, "Dyin's part of livin'. I wouldn't mind havin' my babies here, even if I knew they had to die here."

"You're playin' house now," her mother said. "Wait'll your belly's big and you're sick from havin' the last one. Wait then and see how you feel."

"I won't feel different," she insisted and turned away from her mother. She saw Brazos watching her and walked over to him. She took his arm and drew him outside. "I *do* feel differently than her. I do!"

She was deeply proud of him, for what he was, she was also. He smiled at her, the flash of his teeth white against his shadowed face. "You don't have to tell me,

89

Martha."

She looked around, then said, "Martin didn't come, did he?"

"He wouldn't," Brazos said. "He don't like people."

"That's a pity," she said softly.

CHAPTER NINE

CLEM AND JETHRO OLROYD WENT ACROSS THE DARK valley to their father's cabin and came back with a four-string tenor banjo and a fiddle. The men were outside, drinking from another jug, when the two boys passed between them and went inside.

Jeb McClintock said, "I doggies, we're goin' to have a bit of dancin'."

The men talked it up, then followed McClintock into the big room where the women gathered. Martha had heavy candles thrust into sockets around the room and a flickering light filled the building. Jethro and Clem were sitting on the counter, tuning their instruments with the my-dog-has-fleas method.

"'Weevily Wheat'" Brazos suggested, but a protesting howl pushed it aside.

"'Skip To My Lou,'" Mrs. Sykes said and dried her hands on a thin cloth.

Clem took an experimental saw with his fiddle bow, then pounded his foot and the music began. Jeb McClintock grabbed Jubal Caine's wife and swung her to the tune. Brazos claimed Martha and the whole building rocked with the thump of capering feet. Slippers shuffled on the bare floor and Jethro Olroyd sang the tune in a reedy voice:

A little red wagon painted blue,
A little red wagon painted blue,
A little red wagon painted blue,
Skip to my Lou, my darlin'.

A mule in the cellar kickin' up through,
A mule in the cellar kickin' up through,
A mule in the cellar kickin' up through,
Skip to my Lou, my darlin'.

Chickens in the haystack, shoo, shoo, shoo,
Chickens in the haystack, shoo, shoo, shoo,
Chickens in the haystack, shoo, shoo, shoo,
Skip to my Lou, my darlin'.

Rabbits in the bean patch, two by two,
Rabbits in the bean patch, two by two,
Rabbits in the bean patch, two by two,
Skip to my Lou, my darlin'.

The music sawed to a halt and the dance ended with everyone laughing. Even Mrs. Olroyd smiled for she found that sadness was not the answer; people responded quicker to a smile.

Darkness was growing deeper now and Jeb McClintock went outside and brought in another jug, passing it around. Clem's foot began to tap and Jubal Caine took a final pull before swinging his wife onto the floor. Brazos moved around the whirling dancers and took Martha's arm, steering her outside. The night was cool and there was a ripe wind blowing off the hills, husking across the flats to pelt the building. Inside, feet were drumming on the floor and men laughed; everyone forgot that a week ago men had died.

"People always forget easy, don't they?" Brazos asked.

Martha turned her head to peer at him through the darkness. Night lay in layers over the land and she rested her back against the rough wall. His arm was around her and she was happy.

"What do they forget?"

"Nothing," he said, "I was talking to myself."

Jethro was singing again and Brazos followed the movements of the dancers by the sounds. The whiskey Jethro had drunk changed his voice, causing it to crack as he moved into another stanza:

> *O Charley, he's a fine young man,*
> *O Charley, he's a dandy,*
> *He loves to hug and kiss the girls,*
> *And feed 'em on good candy.*
>
> *The higher up the cherry tree,*
> *The riper are the cherries,*
> *The more you hug and kiss the girls,*
> *The sooner they will marry.*
>
> *My pretty little pink, I suppose you think,*
> *I care but little about you.*
> *But I'll let you know before you go,*
> *I can't do without you.*
>
> *It's left hand 'round your weevily wheat.*
> *It's both hands 'round your weevily wheat.*
> *Come down this way with your weevily wheat.*
> *Oh, swing, Oh, swing, your weevily wheat.*

Laughter was a rising sound, swelling louder as the

door opened and Ray Olroyd staggered out, his face a sickly gray. He saw Brazos and his sister in the darker shadows and grunted, then turned to the wall and was sick. After a few minutes of violent retching, Ray straightened and looked intently at Brazos. "Can't you two wait to get alone?" he asked, his words slurred.

"You're drunk," Martha said harshly. "Leave us alone!"

"Sure," he said and weaved. He stood with his head thrust forward, his legs wide-spread for balance. "Why don't you go off in th' weeds and do your babyin' ? Or has a bed spoiled you, Martha?"

"Damn you—" Brazos began and took a step, but Martha blocked him.

"He's drunk!" She placed her hands against Brazos' chest and flipped her head around to her brother. "Get out of here, Ray! Go on—git!"

The McClintocks came out of the building then, Jubal Caine and Mrs. Olroyd behind them. Light spouted from the open door and they saw these three along the fringes. McClintock moved out of the way and Sykes and his family came out. In a moment they were all outside, gathered in a quiet ring around Brazos Caine and Ray Olroyd.

"What's goin' on here?" McClintock asked. Ray's head came around slowly.

"Private," Olroyd said. "Personal quarrel."

"No quarrel," Brazos said softly. "The man's drunk."

"Drunk or sober," Olroyd said, "I let no man make a whore out of my sister."

"Ray!" Martha's voice was a whip. "That's enough!"

"More than enough," Brazos said and took a step toward Olroyd. Olroyd's hand whipped across his stomach and a knife flashed, but Brazos leaned back and the tip merely ripped his buckskin shirt across the front.

"Put that damn thing away," McClintock said and moved toward Olroyd's right arm, but the young man struck at McClintock and the old man recoiled.

"Don't nobody get near me," Olroyd said, breathing heavily.

"He's tetched," Jubal Caine opined. "Seen likker do that to a man once."

"I ain't tetched," Ray said softly. "I see more'n you all see. I sure do. I see my sister layin' up with him and I know he ain't aimin' to marry her. Not him, he ain't."

"Somebody hit that man with something," Sykes said flatly, but did not volunteer to get within range of the knife.

Brazos pushed Martha behind him and began a slow shuffle around Ray Olroyd. Ray was saying, "You're crippled, but I don't care. I'm drunk and that makes it even. Wouldn't be white to a man, would you? I wanted to help you trap, but you didn't want another man to know you deal with Injuns, did you?" He made a stabbing slash at Brazos' face, then laughed. "Come and get me, Caine. Come in closer and I'll see what your guts look like." He jabbed with the knife, but Brazos stepped aside and the knife missed by an inch.

"I don't want to hurt you, Ray," Brazos said softly, "but I won't put up with no talk about Martha."

"I'm goin' to open you up," Olroyd was saying. "Then I'm goin' to get rich trappin'. Rich, you hear?" He began to sweat and his moccasins scuffed the ground as he moved in a circle, always keeping Brazos before him.

Olroyd was not as drunk as he had seemed and Brazos guessed that Ray had been putting on a good act. The wind of caution blew gently against Brazos and he

94

measured his chances and found them slim. His right arm was too sore to wield a knife and he was not good enough with his left. To grapple with Olroyd was his best bet, but exceedingly risky considering Olroyd's knife.

Olroyd said, "You got no guts, Caine. All them lies I hear about you fightin' Comanches—nothin' but damn lies. You'd pee if you ever saw a Comanche close."

"For God sake!" Sykes said. "Can't somebody do somethin'?"

"Why don't you shut your mouth?" his wife asked. "You stop him if you're so brave."

Olroyd was beginning to tire of this and he made a thrusting lunge. Brazos slipped to one side and the two men reversed positions, pivoting to face each other. Brazos stepped in and the knife jerked, then came back to the guard position. Stamping his foot suddenly, Brazos ducked the sweeping blade. Quickly, he was on Olroyd's back, one arm fending off the knife as it whipped back, trying to reach his face. The steel bit through the sleeve and drew blood in Brazos' forearm, then he had the arm imprisoned, the other around Olroyd's throat, shutting off the wind.

Straining, Olroyd tried to throw Brazos off his back by planting his feet solidly and thrashing his body about, but Brazos clung to him, a steel clamp around Olroyd's throat.

The pain in Brazos' shoulder was making him sick, but he could not release Olroyd's knife arm. Olroyd's legs were growing weaker and they bent like soft wax. He made deep strangling noises as he fell completely. Retaining his throat hold, Brazos wrenched the knife from Olroyd and then threw the man flat on his back.

While Brazos had fought, he had not been angry, but

95

now a deep-rooted rage filled him. The light streaming from the door fell on him as he squatted on Olroyd's chest, the knife poised.

"No!" Martha screamed this and the sound penetrated his anger like a knife splitting cloth. He began to tremble. Instead of sinking the knife in Olroyd's throat, he cut the man's buckskin pants from hip to ankle, then stood up.

Olroyd was choking and drawing great sobs of air. Brazos pulled him to his feet by the hair. Olroyd's pants fell off and he stood in the light with nothing on but his shirt. The women gasped and turned while Jeb McClintock's booming laugh rolled out into the night.

Realizing that they were laughing at him, Olroyd tried to hit Brazos. Brazos struck Olroyd on the side of the head with the flat part of the blade and knocked him down. He kicked Olroyd's bare buttocks and said, "Now crawl away from here like a damn dog!"

Starting out on his hands and knees, Olroyd presented a ludicrous figure and gales of laughter followed him. Then he got to his feet and began to run. Brazos flung the bowie knife after him, then turned to the gathering.

They broke up immediately, the women chattering and the men saying how funny Ray had looked on his hands and knees. Brazos stood there, sweat a-shine on his face. His shoulder ached like blazes. He found Martha waiting by the door. The others were on their way across the valley.

"You were going to kill him, weren't you?"

"Yes," he admitted.

"Why, Brazos? Because of what he said?"

"I guess." She was a silhouette with the light behind her and he wished she would move so he could see her face.

"I think you were angry because you believed him," she said.

"I didn't say that," he countered quickly.

"You didn't have to. Is it so important to be first with me?"

"Maybe it is," he admitted. "I'm not like Martin, a squaw in every camp."

"I know," she said, "but suppose you weren't first?"

"Don't ask me somethin' I can't answer. I never thought of it."

"But Ray made you think of it," she said. "You hope he's lyin', don't you?"

He made a fanning motion with his hands. "Martha, do you have to rag a man? I just felt like cuttin' his throat, that's all."

She came away from the door and kissed him, her face soft in the candlelight. "I've got to go if I expect to catch your mother and father."

He took her arm. "You're not mad at me, Martha?"

"It's all right," she said softly and was gone. He stared at the empty, silent yard and went around the large building to his cabin. The fireplace glowed redly and he lay down on his bed, staring at the inky rafters. The emptiness of the place was like a tomb and an engulfing loneliness became his companion.

Rain fell intermittently for the next week and then the sky broke apart and the sunshine made brilliant slashes through the clouds. Steam began to rise from the ground in dense layers and the raw dampness finally faded away.

That afternoon Martin and Emma walked through the settlement, not stopping at Ryker's, but came on to Brazos' cabin. Martha was in the yard making soap.

She had a caldron hung over a hot fire and was mixing grease and lye. Raising her head, she saw them coming across the flats and called to Brazos, who was in the store constructing shelves.

Martin went into the store while Emma went into the cabin with Martha. Martin said, "You still mean to go to Fort Davis?"

"I mean to take my wagons through," Brazos said. "The oxen are at Pa's and I'll have to hitch up."

"Well now," Martin said and rubbed his face, "I hadn't considered that." He looked around the store building. "Seems that you was doin' more than flappin' your mouth." He blew out a long breath. "I'll leave my woman here with yours. She won't be safe alone."

"Th' Comanches seem quiet enough," Brazos said. "That lickin' they took hurt."

"Ain't th' Comanches I worry about," Martin said. "That Emma's got her charms, dogged if she ain't, and Ray Olroyd's noticed it. He's been around my place; I seen sign."

"He ain't been near th' settlement since th' housewarmin'," Brazos said.

He walked across the flats to his father's place and led the string of oxen to Ryker's lean-to. There he yoked them in pairs to eight Mexican carts. They were crude, compared to an Eastern-made wagon, but in country where there were no roads, they were very practical. The base was solid plank and the solid wheels were bound by heavy steel rims. Hardwood stakes lashed together formed the sideboards, but they could carry a ton apiece over impossible ground.

Unlike horses, oxen were no problem. Roped into a line, they followed the leader. Pulling the caravan over to his cabin, Brazos loaded two carts from his hide loft,

98

then loaded two more from Ryker's hide shed. These were all the pelts he owned, close to three thousand dollars worth. Ryker stood in the doorway while Brazos lashed down the last bale. Ryker said, "That wipes out your damn credit here, Brazos. I'll hold no more of your plunder, the way you're treatin' me—selfish-like."

Brazos smiled and looked up as Martha came across the flats, his sleeping robes and pistols slung over her shoulder. She put the food in the first cart and waited until he had buckled his weapons around his waist.

"How long will you be gone?"

"Three weeks to a month," he said. He thought of something then, and added, "My rifle's over th' mantel. Keep it handy."

A smile flitted across her lips. "You're not worried, are you?"

"A man who protects what's his never needs to worry," he said. Martin went into Ryker's then and Brazos looked after him. "How come Emma didn't come with you?"

"She didn't want to," Martha said. "Is she afraid of him Brazos?"

"How would I know?" he said. "Why don't you ask her?"

"I intend to," she said and kissed him before turning back to his cabin.

Ryker and Martin were in the barroom and Ryker had the jug out. Brazos came up and leaned against the bar. "I hate to take empty wagons," he said, looking at Ryker. "You help me load 'em?"

Ryker was all smiles now and he hopped over the bar. "I knew you'd help me out," he said. "When you get there see that I get top price. Find out when the militia train's comin' through."

"A week ago you didn't think anyone could make it," Brazos said. "You change your mind?"

"You're pickin' at me," Ryker accused. "I got two hundred dollars worth of grain there. Bring me back some whiskey, boy."

"No whiskey," Brazos said. "Some of these people drink their credits up and let their women and kids go hungry." He turned and hooked his elbows on the bar. "Vrain and Gooding's got a shipment waitin' for me. Ordered it last year. I got pots, pans, tools, barreled staples, cloth—I even got needles. A man wants his drink, then let him run a still. I don't sell blue ruin in my place."

"By God, these goods's mine," Ryker said. "If I want half my money in whiskey, then you bring me whiskey."

"All right," Brazos said and went in the storeroom to load the remaining carts.

Three hours later they left the valley behind them, plodded up the gentle slope of the hillside and angled north. Once Ryker's was out of sight, the caravan moved with the dip of the land and they held to this achingly slow pace until the sun dipped toward the horizon. During the dark hours, Brazos began to follow the higher slopes and much later indicated their camp site in a cup of rocks and stunted timber.

The camp was high and cold and there was no fire. They ate jerky from their possible sacks and sat around, silence between them like a wall.

Finally Brazos said, "Emma'll make you a good wife, Martin."

The man grunted softly, his face turning toward Brazos. "I've had better, you can bet on that."

"She kept you home for two weeks. Never seen a

100

squaw who could do that to you."

"I'm not home now, am I?" Martin paused. "You stickin' your nose in my business?"

"Nope. Just makin' talk."

"I don't like to talk," Martin said and lay back on his robes.

The night was dark and clear; small animals moved about on their nocturnal business. Brazos listened to the soft murmur of life around him. A cessation of these sounds would mean that they were no longer alone in the vastness.

"You didn't buy her for a string of beads and a spotted pony," Brazos said. "Don't treat her like a squaw, Martin."

The mountain man came to his hands and knees, peering through the darkness at Brazos. "Don't tell me what to do. I claimed her and no man'll interfere, you understand? I never seen the like of her in no woman. I remember my first squaw, a Pawnee she was. I fought her every time I took her. Couldn't turn my back on her lest she knife me. They all been that way, hatin' you even when you was givin' 'em a good time. But Emma ain't like that and it perplexes a man. She's never raised a claw to me and I don't rightly understand it. Makes a man wonder what's in a woman's head."

Martin sighed and rolled over. Brazos sat on his robes, hunched over against the mounting chill. Near midnight he shook Martin, bringing him instantly awake.

He took a position above the camp while Brazos rolled into his robe and slept. The first light of dawn awakened him and they ate a cold meal before going on. Martin was in a darkly taciturn mood and Brazos made no attempt to speak.

101

In a limited way, Brazos understood Martin. They were bound together by a common understanding of the land. Never friendliness, for Martin called no man friend. Brazos often wondered if Martin had ever known the softness of a mother's hand, or if he had known it, recalled it. He could recall the tight spots they had been in and out of and never once did Martin ever turn to Brazos as a friend. Martin fought for himself and no one else. He was a companion only because he needed a good man; he had selected Brazos as calmly as a man selects a new rifle.

These pieces of understanding Brazos had pieced together from the miles they had traveled. He turned his head now and looked toward the rear of the caravan. Martin walked alone, his rifle across his chest.

The man was alone with his thoughts, as he had always been.

CHAPTER TEN

FOR TEN DAYS THEY TRAVELED NORTH, KEEPING TO THE protection of the land. There seemed no end to the mountains until the morning of the sixth day when they breasted the last ridge and looked upon the clutter of buildings surrounded by a stout palisade in the valley below.

Fort Davis was small. The palisade walls were no more than a hundred yards long on each side. Behind the fort, a small settlement bloomed, full of ambitious Americans, a few friendly Indians from the Staked Plains country and Mexicans. Within the confines of the palisade were the militia buildings, and the sutler's store. The militia comprised the bulk, long billets for the troops, three supply buildings, a farrier's shed, and the regimental headquarters.

By mid-morning Brazos led his caravan off the slopes and moved across the flats toward the palisade gates. A militiaman walked the rampart with a rifle on his shoulder. He saw them and stood ready. The sergeant-of-the-guard was called and he recognized them. The gates swung open.

They crossed the parade and halted before Vrain and Gooding's trading post. Brazos went inside, Martin trailing along behind him.

Joshua Vrain was tending counter, a bear of a man with dark eyes and a booming voice. His whiskers bristled thick and undisciplined. He held out his arms in welcome. "Well, well," he said. "I figured you poor bastards were dead by this time." He shot Martin a glance. "Not you. You're too damned mean to get killed."

"Got a mess of plews and grain for you to look at," Brazos said, leaning against the counter.

"That so? You'n Martin in business now?"

"He's in business," Martin said. "I come along to get away from th' damn settlement."

"One of these days," Vrain prophesied, "you're goin' to kill off all the damn Injuns, then where'll you be? The only thing left will be to bite yourself and commit suicide." He produced a jug from beneath the counter. "Let's have a hooker before we get to talkin' business." He grinned at Brazos. "I think I could whip you."

He reached across the counter and Brazos grabbed him. Vrain planted his feet solidly, but Brazos had him by the beard. Whirling, he placed his back to the counter and hauled Vrain over his shoulder. Both men hit the floor with stunning impact, but Brazos was on top, both fists in Vrain's whiskers. A good crowd was jamming the doorway and Brazos banged Vrain's head on the floor twice, then got up laughing.

Rising to his hands and knees, Vrain felt tenderly of his cheeks. "Goddamned catamount anyway! You're half-horse'n half-alligator." He climbed back over the counter. "Let's get back to the whiskey." He shoved the jug toward Martin who scowled and snapped, "I don't want your goddamned liquor!"

He wheeled and rammed his way through the crowd at the door. Vrain stared after him. "What the hell's he on the peck about?"

"A woman. Got himself a woman and he ain't figured her out yet."

Vrain shook his head. "They'll do that to a man. Come on, drink up."

"I'll get my tradin' done first," Brazos said lazily. "You're a damn pirate when you get corn in your belly and I aim to get tit for tat."

Vrain winked at the men gathered in the store. "This young hoss is smarter'n I figured." He pushed the jug aside. "All right, let's go see them plews. Your stuff come in three months ago. I thought I was goin' to make a double profit on it, seein's how you already paid for it."

Outside, Brazos and four militiamen unloaded the wagons and Vrain went over the pelts, complaining in a dry voice. Brazos sagged against a porch upright and talked to several men while Vrain tallied the goods. Finally he straightened and said, "Eight hundred for the grain. Not a damn cent more." He stroked his whiskers. "I'll go twenty-five hundred on the pelts, though."

"Go to blazes," Brazos said.

"Jesus! You want the blood from a man's veins? I got to make a profit and the market's down."

"Th' market's always down, to hear you tell it," Brazos said. "Three even on the plews. I'm comin' through regular now, Vrain. Got me a store of my own and a goodly business if you'll come my way a little."

Vrain clasped his head in both hands and rocked it back and forth, his eyes rolled upward. "Twenty-eight and that's my best offer. I'm doin' you a turn at that price."

"Guess I'll have to go on to Austin," Brazos said smoothly. "I can eliminate the middle man that way, which is you, Vrain."

"All right," Vrain said. "Drink my blood then. Three on the pelts and nine hundred on the grain. But a thousand of that in trade."

"Agreed," Brazos said and turned back into the store. Vrain had the goods carried to the storeroom and Brazos began to pick his supplies. He selected seed, jugs of vinegar, eight tubs of lye, powder, caps, needles, twenty bolts of cloth and twenty boxes of dried fruits. He did not get any whiskey for Ryker.

Brazos was a shrewd trader. What he lacked in formal education he made up for with his understanding of human nature. The largest percentage of his goods was for the women, dresses from New Orleans, shoes and boots with copper toes, scented soap, sewing gear and glass for windows. He had tools, tobacco, rice, new firearms and work clothing. But he counted heavily on the women. They had gone without and would want these things. He knew how much trouble a discontented woman could be and he felt confident that he would sell out in a short time.

Vrain had a new shipment of coal-oil lamps and Brazos bought two dozen of these for three dollars apiece, plus four casks of coal-oil. In his mind's eye, he

105

could see a lamp shining in every window in the settlement. No woman would rest until she had one on her table, even if she had to drive her husband to get it.

Mid-afternoon saw his goods loaded and the wagons standing by the quartermaster sheds. Then he walked across the parade ground to the headquarters building. A militiaman ushered him into Captain Travers' office.

"I haven't heard from the Bend country in over a year," Travers said. He was a spare man with the weight of command heavy on him. His office was spartan, the walls planked with rough-sawed lumber. "Sorry as hell about the supply trains, Caine, but we made two attempts to get through. I lost nine men on that detail and I couldn't risk another." He sighed and bit off the end of a cigar. "Beats the hell out of me how you do it."

"We don't make much noise," Brazos said. "Martin's pretty good in the hills."

Travers looked up quickly. "Did he come with you?"

"Yes. Somethin' wrong?"

"I don't want him on the post," Travers said flatly. He put a light to his cigar and blew a thin cloud of smoke toward the ceiling. "Got some movers for you, Brazos. They're in the settlement waitin' for a guide to take 'em through."

"To the Bend country?"

Travers shook his head. "They want to go further west." He got up and walked over to the side door that opened onto the parade. A militiaman walked by and Travers stopped him. "Find Martin, if he's on the post. Tell him to get out or I'll have him locked up."

The man saluted and Travers came back in. "I've always hated to tell a man he's licked, Brazos, but let's face it; the Bend country is uninhabitable. You're too close to Mexico and the Comanche stronghold. I recommend that you return, gather the remaining families and bring them out. There's land on the Trinity and Colorado—good land."

"There's only nine families left."

"Jesus God! Two years ago there were twenty-some." He shook his head. "You're in rough country without a road or a good trail that's passable all year around. You and Martin manage to get through, but I can't with a troop. Give it up; that's sound advice."

"McClintock would like to see us fortify," Brazos said.

"McClintock?" Travers frowned. "Oh, yes—the Kentucky fire-eater. What does he mean? Was Ryker burned out?"

"No, but we need cannon, Captain. With cannons mounted on the corners of the settlement house, we could keep the Comanches back."

Travers pulled at his mustaches. "Caine, how in the hell would you get 'em back if I let you have 'em? There's powder and shot to think about too."

Brazos pulled at his ear. "You give me the big guns and I'll find some way to get 'em back."

"I'll let you have four," Travers said and offered his hand. "I'll leave a message with the ordnance sergeant. Contact him any time if you work out something."

Brazos went out and crossed the parade again to the main gate. He skirted the palisade wall and entered the settlement behind the fort. There was just one street with a dozen small buildings flanking it. To the right, the mover's camp was partially screened by cottonwoods along the creek. Brazos altered his course and approached the wagons. They were a sorry lot, too heavy-wheeled for tough mountain trails, and they were in poor shape. A bearded man had been mending

107

harness and now he put this aside to stand up.

"I'm Brazos Caine from the Bend country. You folks lookin' for land?"

"Yes," the man said. "Name's Modry. This is my train. Come straight across this spring from Orleans. What's in the Bend country?"

"Land's there," Brazos told him. "Trouble too. Indians, Mexicans, but it suits me. You spread it around that I'm leavin' in the mornin' with my supply train. We'd be glad to have you."

"Kind of late in the year to be movin'," Modry said carefully. He was hairy-faced and his clothes were well worn. "A man hates to jump into somethin'."

"You'd be no worse off," Brazos declared, "than you are now. Livin' out of a wagon ain't my idea of livin' at all. Leastways we got a settlement and a few buildin's."

"I'll think on it," Modry promised. "Come for supper; my woman's a good cook."

"Thanks, I will," Brazos said. He walked up the settlement street and considered the possibilities. Modry, and perhaps the other men, were satisfied to winter out here, but the women wanted four walls and a roof over their heads. To Brazos, it was a predictable thing. A woman would harp at her man until he gave her four walls and the roof.

They'll go, he thought and paused to look the single street over. The buildings were log, mud-chinked. Flat, dirty buildings without glass in the windows and rawhide hinges supporting the doors. The cantina was on the corner and the door stood open. A few Mexicans hung around by the door and an old Indian sat hunched over, a blanket around his bony shoulders.

Going inside, Brazos saw Martin leaning against the bar, a gold piece in his hand. There was an exchange of

Spanish between Martin and the bartender, then a jug changed hands.

Martin took a table by the wall and Brazos crossed the room. He toed a stool around and sat across from Martin. When Martin drank, trickles ran past the corners of his mouth. He lowered the jug and coughed. Tears stood out in his eyes and his voice was hoarse when he spoke.

"I feel like hell and when I feel that way, I don't give a goddamn for nothin', not even you, Brazos."

"You never did," Brazos said evenly. "Did you ever call a man 'friend,' Martin?"

"No," Martin said sullenly and upended the jug again. "Better get out of here, 'cause I'm goin' to get roarin' drunk and I'm not fit to be with when I'm drunk."

"You ain't fit to be with when you're sober," Brazos said frankly. "You ought to go out and kill an Indian so you'll feel better."

Martin's hand came across the table and fastened onto Brazos' shirt, half-pulling the young man off the stool. "S'matter with you? Your own brother and sister killed, but you don't care. Why don't you hate?" He tried to shake Brazos. "Why don't you?"

He let go of the shirt to take another drink. "Goddamn little slut, that's what she is. Lovin' me all th' damn time. Makin' me feel like a dirty animal afterward." His eyes were bloodshot. "Stealin' from me, that's what she's doin', th' little whore. Got no love for a woman, see. Clay an' me didn't need no woman, you understand. Come and go as we pleased, Clay and me did. Didn't need no pink-assed slut to make us happy."

Brazos watched Martin and a glimmer of understanding came to him. He stood up, saying, "Why don't you go out and get killed?"

109

Martin raised his head and stared, then Brazos turned and walked out. Pouring another slug down his throat, Martin set the jug aside and rested his heavy forearms on the rough table. Men drifted in and out, but he paid no attention. There were a few Mexicans standing at one end of the bar, while farther down, two mountain men passed a jug back and forth between them.

Outside, the remaining daylight dwindled and a Mexican girl came from the back room with a taper and lighted the candles. Martin followed her with his eyes, watching the movement of her buttocks as she walked. His interest quickened.

When she passed close he reached out and imprisoned her wrist. Her eyes met his, level and faintly smiling. He said, "There's some left in the jug, sweetheart."

She raised an eyebrow and spoke in soft Spanish. Then she sat down. Her hand reached out for the gold pieces he had lying between the triangle of his forearms. Martin pushed her hand away.

"Nonononono," he said softly. "You got a price? You all have." She cocked her head to one side, not understanding. He pushed two of the gold pieces toward her, but kept his hand on them. A new speculation came into the girl's eyes and she leaned forward so that the blouse fell away from her breasts. She placed her hand over his, completely covering the gold pieces.

Martin put his weight against the table and stood up, swaying a little. The girl took his arm and they left the barroom, moving down a darkened hall. Martin was mumbling. "You just want money, don't ya? No holdin' a man, stealin' from him. Jus' a little money, tha's all you ask, ain't it? Women steal love—you know that? Take it 'fore a man knows it's gone."

In her room she shrugged out of her skirt and blouse, pulling him to her with practised hands. Her voice was a low, purring sound while out in the bar one of the mountain men whooped in a ringing voice and laughter filtered into this small, dark room.

She moved against him with professional skill and through the haze of the whiskey he had consumed, a wild anger began to invade his mind. He jerked away from her, striking for her face. The girl yelped in pained surprise and Martin staggered against the wall, fumbling for the door.

In the barroom, the yellow candlelight made him blink. He searched for his jug but it was gone. He faced the bartender full of belligerence. The Mexican behind the bar waited, a finely held caution in his eyes.

He grinned weakly and said, "Was the plum not ripe, *señor*? I heard her cry out."

"Who took my whiskey?" Martin said thickly. There was no humor in his eyes and his hands moved aimlessly.

"I do not know, *señor*," the Mexican said. Slyly, he shot a glance down the bar where the mountain men stood.

Martin caught this and drew his own drunken conclusions. He turned to the two men and said, "Give me back my likker or I'll open your damned guts!"

CHAPTER ELEVEN

BECAUSE HE WAS WORRIED ABOUT MARTIN, BRAZOS returned to the cantina shortly after dark. He stepped into the doorway and stopped there, for Martin was challenging the two mountain men. On Martin's face

111

was an ugliness that went deeper than mere expression. Martin said, "You hear me? I'll split you like a shoat!"

One of the men, a tall, rail-lean man, said, "He wants a fuss."

Brazos stepped deeper into the room then and said, "I'll take care of him. He's drunk."

The mountain men did not look at Brazos when he spoke. "Never you mind, hoss. Your friend's bought himself somethin'." To Martin, he said, "Well, hoss, if you've got your mind set on somethin', best get it off."

"Son'vabitch," Martin said. "You scared to fight?"

"Now, hoss," the man said, shooting his friend a quick grin, "we got a feller here who's just rilin' for a whoop-up." He stepped away from the bar and rolled his shoulders, the fringe on his sleeves stirring. "Been out a smart spell myself and I guess I'll go you a reel or two. But no knives! I hate a cuttin' fight worse'n poison."

"This won't be for fun," Martin said and took off his belt containing his weapons. The tall man shed his powder horn, cap box and knife, laying these on the bar alongside of Martin's gear.

They moved together by common consent, both delivering ear-splitting whoops as they collided.

Martin hit the tall man in the chest with his fist, laughing wildly as he followed him down. Hooking an arm around Martin's neck, the tall man laced him stiffly in the mouth before releasing him.

Martin was strong and agile as a cat. He struck the tall man a glancing blow as they struggled to their feet. Then he whipped up a stool and broke it across the tall man's back. The tall man went down, but in doing so, reached out and pulled both of Martin's feet from under him. The Mexican bartender began to call on God to

112

intervene and the two men rolled on the floor, still whooping loudly.

Martin was bleeding from the nose and mouth; the tall man had one eye nearly closed.

They bore into each other, arms windmilling. For a full minute they battered each other, then Martin swung and missed and while he was off balance, the tall man connected.

The impact of fist on bone was like a stick whipped into mud; then Martin fell and lay still. Throughout the fight, the other mountain man had remained by the bar. Now he came over and looked at Martin. "Reckon we ought to stand the hoss a drink," he said.

The Mexican was lamenting his smashed stool but one of the mountain men gave him a level stare and the whining stopped. Brazos went behind the bar and lifted an oak pail of water. He dumped this in Martin's face and watched him sputter.

From the back room the Mexican girl came to the doorway and looked without interest upon the scene. One side of her face was bruised.

"How did this start?" Brazos asked.

"He's seen too many hills," the tall man said. "A man gets like that once in a while."

Martin was on his feet now. The blood had stopped dripping from his nose, but streaks of it stayed on his cheeks like warpaint. He turned to the bar and put on his weapons belt.

"He had a jug and some gold when I left him," Brazos said. "Where is it?"

"The Mex got the jug," the tall man said. He nodded toward the girl. "Reckon she got the gold."

Brazos looked at the woman, then whipped his eyes to Martin. A full understanding came to him and he

113

said, "Get out of here, Martin!"

"Don't toss me," Martin said. He looked at Brazos and saw the unfriendliness there. "Now don't ask for trouble, Brazos."

Brazos approached him like a stiff-legged dog and then hit Martin with shocking suddenness. The blow contained pent-up fury and power and Martin was whipped completely around by it. He fell back almost out the door and Brazos stalked him. He lifted Martin by the collar and dragged him into the dark street.

A horse trough stood nearby and Brazos dumped Martin into it. The man came up, water cascading from his hair and clothes. Brazos put his foot on the stone edge and said, "Martin, you want to fight me now? I'll fight you. Pistols, rifles, a knife—anything you want?"

Martin shook his head from side to side. "Don't want to fight. Don't want nothin'."

"Fight me now or never," Brazos said, "because I'm through with you, you understand? *Through!* You're no goddamned good, Martin. You're rotten inside, eaten up with somethin' nobody understands. So you wanted Clay to be somethin'? So you never forgot him—to hell with all that! You're a crazy man, Martin. People have told me, but I never paid it no mind. Now I've had enough. Emma loved you but that wasn't enough for you. You got to crawl in with some slut as soon's you get the chance. Well, go on! Do as you damned please. Go out and kill yourself a damn Indian—that's all you live for, to kill somethin'!"

Martin stared at him. Then he reached out a hand and Brazos knocked it aside. "Just keep your distance. I don't know what's eatin' you, but it might be catchin'."

Brazos turned and started to walk away. "Wait! I— I'm mixed up, kid. All mixed up like a damn curd," choked Martin.

"Who gives a damn?" Brazos said. "We're headin' back in the mornin'. Come or not, it makes no difference to me." He walked away, his moccasins scuffing the dirt.

He went back to the mover's camp and squatted by the fire. Modry handed him a cup of coffee and he drank in silence, then shied the grounds into the fire when he was through.

"Decided yet, Modry?"

Men began to drift near Modry's fire and Brazos looked at them. Their faces were no different from the faces at Ryker's settlement and this surprised him. They were, he saw, the faces of men who worked the land, patient, drawn faces, full of lines and trouble.

Modry said, "We'll go. The women want a roof over 'em and a man has to provide what's necessary."

"There's one thing," Brazos said. "I'm takin' four cannon and enough powder and shot to do a job along with me. Now I got no room, so I was wonderin' if we couldn't find room in your wagons."

"I don't know," Modry said and stroked his beard "We're full up as it is. Carted this stuff a long way. Some as far as Ohio."

"The cannon *have* to go back with me," Brazos stated. "We'll have to make room some way. Shift stuff around until we get room."

"How much them cannon weigh?" one man asked, his jaws working on a cud of tobacco.

"Nearly four hundred pounds apiece," Brazos said. "A hundred balls is another three hundred, plus a hundred and fifty in powder."

"That's a heap of weight," Modry said slowly. He had a habit of speaking with a short silence between each word.

"You got some light wagons," Brazos said. "We could take some of the goods out and load it in the heavy wagons."

Modry considered it, then turned to a short, muscular man. "What's your 'pinion, Chase?"

Chase spoke to Brazos. "Be these cannon really necessary?"

"I'll pay twenty dollars in gold to every man who furnishes a wagon," Brazos said. "We've been fightin' with rifles and lettin' the Comanches come to us. With these cannon on th' corners of my tradin' post, I could keep the valley clear."

"For twenty dollars I can make room," Chase said. "You want this done tonight?"

"Now," Brazos told him. "Take off the canvas an' bows. I'll be waitin' at the powder magazine for you."

Modry nodded and the meeting broke up. Brazos re-entered the post. He found Captain Travers by the guard station at the main gate. A heavy storm lantern hung on each side of the hinge poles, casting a feeble puddle of light on the ground.

Travers said, "Brazos, you still want those cannon?"

"There's wagons comin' in to load 'em."

Travers turned and paced Brazos across the parade. He asked, "What was the trouble Martin got into at the settlement?"

"Somethin' personal," Brazos hedged. He glanced at Travers, but darkness shrouded the captain's face. "Why don't you want Martin on the post, Captain?"

"He killed an Indian."

"He's killed lots of Indians."

"Not like he killed this one," Travers said. "Did you know his brother, Clay?"

116

"Not good," Brazos admitted.

The sentries walked their palisade posts, the call going around to post number one, then fading. Travers walked on a few paces in silence. "Clay and Martin were close; Clay was Martin's whole life. They were up on the Yellowstone ten years ago; Clay was no more than a kid then. Martin was a slave to him. Did everythin' for him. Fought his fights, wiped his damned nose."

"You didn't think much of Clay?"

"Tell me anyone who did," Travers said. "Everybody hated his guts, except Martin. Clay was all mouth, always talkin' about what he and Martin would do together. Jealous as a damned woman, he was. Martin'd get tired after a while and take himself a squaw. Clay would bust it up. The story went around that Clay killed a Blackfoot woman of Martin's when he was away, then said she died of the fever."

From the shadows of the powder magazine a musket rattled as a trooper brought it to the ready, then the man recognized Captain Travers and came to attention. "At ease," Travers said and unlocked the magazine. He squatted in the darkness by the wall and the trooper went to the other side of the building. Travers went on in a soft voice. "Clay was always able to convince Martin that everybody was wrong and that Clay was right. He got away with it too. When Ryker began the settlement, Clay hated everybody, especially McClintock because the old man wouldn't take Clay's sass. From th' first, it looked like someone was sellin' the settlers out. The Comanches would raid when the folks was away, or in th' fields. Seemed uncanny how they'd know." Travers sighed. "We was makin' a few patrols through there then. I seen my share of it."

117

"Sell out?" Brazos said. "What th' hell for?"

"For nothing," Travers said. "Some men are odd when it comes to havin' somethin' for themselves. They squat on a piece of land and don't want no one to come near 'em."

"That ain't no reason for a man to—"

Travers held up his hand. "Clay began to preach to Martin, tellin' him how McClintock was out to get him, makin' up lies that McClintock was supposed to have said. And all th' time Clay was tradin' heavy with Esqueda, and cheatin' him blind. Him and Martin would bring stuff in from Orleans; I guess Comanches got their trade rifles from Clay."

"McClintock fought with Esqueda," Brazos said. "Captain, Clay never had anythin' to do with that."

"You think he didn't? He'd fill McClintock's ear about Esqueda, then go across th' river and tell Esqueda that McClintock hated all Mexicans. McClintock didn't know what was goin' on and when Esqueda came to talk, there was a hassle. Esqueda come to me with the story, exactly as I'm tellin' you. I guess I said somethin' while puttin' two and two together, because when Clay went back across the river to make his deals with the Comanches, he just never come back."

"Martin thinks Esqueda killed him."

"Esqueda or Comanches. They both had reasons. Even an Indian hates to be sold out, and Clay'd sell anybody out. Anyway he's dead and it was enough to set Martin goin'."

"Comanches got nothin' a man can use," Brazos said.

"They can steal," Travers said. "Mexicans got gold, boy, and Clay had a weakness for it. Some men can shake your hand and stab you at th' same time."

"Martin wasn't like that," Brazos said. "He's a hater,

118

Captain, but he ain't *that* way. It was easy to guess he wanted to get even with Esqueda, but he's done that a long time ago. I guess I know him as good as any man, and yet I don't know him at all."

"You two always made a strange pair," Travers said, "and I've wondered about that. You know there's been others wonderin' too. He's not your friend, Brazos. You know that?"

"Sure," Brazos said softly. "But I guess he wants to be. Seems like he wants to powerful bad, but he just don't know how."

"Martin's gone too far along the road to turn back," Travers said. "I've seen this before. I went up the Missouri in '31. I've seen men who were wild, animal-wild. Like Martin is. A man keeps his mind locked on one thing, like revenge, and it eats away the rest until there's nothin' worth savin'. Martin lives just so's he can kill another man. I've seen this, how it turns out. Couldn't talk to 'em about anythin' and you sure as hell couldn't trust 'em. They'd sit around a fire with the whites of their eyes showin' and watch you. You say some little thing and out'd come their knife and they'd rip you. Martin's gettin' like that. I saw it the night he killed the Indian in Vrain and Gooding's place. No reason for it. He just upped and decided that he'd kill something."

"He's taken a woman," Brazos said. "Jeb McClintock's girl. He's never looked at a white woman before her."

"The color of her hide won't matter," Travers said.

The guards at the main gate called out and then swung wide to admit the four wagons. Travers rose from his position and spoke to the sentry. "My compliments to Sergeant McGruger. Tell him to report on the double with the three-man detail."

The sentry ran across the parade toward the darkened barracks and the wagons parked by the powder magazine. Travers lit a storm lantern and hung it by the door. Sergeant McGruger appeared with his men and Travers said, "Sergeant, rig an 'A' frame here and load four three-pounders into these wagons. A hundred rounds of powder and ball goes with it. See that they have rammers and swabs."

McGruger hustled his men into the dugout. The "A" frame was set up outside the door so the wagons could back under it. The cannon were mounted on small four-wheeled trunnions and McGruger and his men wrestled these to the door where slings were fastened.

In an hour the cannon were loaded and secured. The cannon balls were stowed and the powder bags packed beneath the seats. Modry and his men mounted and drove slowly from the post while Travers dismissed McGruger's detail.

Taking the lantern, he walked back across the parade with Brazos Caine. "Where are you putting up tonight?"

"Horse Barns," Brazos told him.

"There's an empty bed in my quarters," Travers said. "Lieutenant McKimmie is on patrol and won't be back until Thursday. You're welcome to use it."

"That's kind," Brazos said and walked with him to the officer's picket quarters. Travers lighted several candles and stripped off his heavy boots. There was a tin stove in the corner and he heated water for his shave.

Brazos took off his buckskin shirt and went outside to wash. When he came back in, Travers was facing a cracked mirror and flicking lather off his razor. "I've got to hand it to you," Travers said, his mouth canted to pull his cheek tight. "I don't think you're going to get through with those wagons, but I admire you just for trying." He turned his head and looked at Brazos. "You want to join the militia? You can read and write; I'll make you a lieutenant."

Brazos grinned. "I'm a trader."

"Big ambition," Travers conceded and went back to his shaving. When he finished and had put the razor away, Brazos had turned to face the wall and was sound asleep. Travers looked at the young man for a moment, then spoke softly. "Not much bothers 'em when they're young."

He glanced again into the mirror and studied the reflection. At thirty-seven his face was weather-whipped and lined around the eyes and forehead. He tried to recall how it had been when he was twenty-one and gave up.

With a sigh, Captain Travers blew out the lamp and eased himself into his own bunk.

CHAPTER TWELVE

WATCHING THE SUNSET FROM THE DOORWAY OF Brazos Caine's cabin, Martha Olroyd decided that here was a beauty that matched the fury of the land. These sunsets were different from any others she had ever seen. Against the higher mountains, bold pennants of color streaked the sky, dyeing it a deep ruby with wild slashes of crimson and purple high against the cloud base. There seemed no gentle diffusion of hue here. Bright tones clashed with conflicting shades and the picture thus wrought was magnificent.

Emma Martin came from the cabin, drying her hands on her apron. She squinted at the sky, then said, "I should be pinin' for him, but I ain't." She gave Martha a sidelong glance. "I guess that's wrong, thinkin' like that."

"Not if that's the way you feel," Martha said.

"He ain't a lovin' man," Emma confided. "I want him to be, but he ain't. Seems that he just don't need me, or anybody else."

"We all need somebody," Martha told her. "He's wild and you'll have to tame him. Women have done it before."

For a moment Emma remained stonily silent, then she said, "I expect I'll be rockin' a cradle soon enough." Martha whipped her head around to look at her and Emma sat down on the stoop.

A grayness was creeping over the land, the outrider for the night, and Emma wished that it would hurry and mask the feeling she knew was plain on her face. Martha said, "Havin' a baby is like plantin'. I guess it's a hard thing for a woman to lose 'em, but all the seeds don't grow to bear fruit. I've stopped cryin' over the thought of dyin'."

"Getting' old's what I hate most," Emma said.

"Old is a long way off, Emma."

"I don't mean natural old," Emma said. "Havin' a baby every year or sooner's what I mean. Sick all th' time and frettin' 'cause you got a new ache every time the weather changes. We got no time to live. Just work. That's th' kind of old I mean, the hurryin' kind where you're plumb wore out at thirty and just tryin' to live one more year so's you'll be thirty-one."

"I see," Martha said softly. "Have you told this to Martin?"

"You don't tell nothin' to Martin. He just grunts when he wants you and you'd better come quick too. I wouldn't bother him with my foolish notions." She tipped her head back and looked at Martha, trying to see through the sooty darkness. "You'd tell your man what you was thinkin', wouldn't you? Pa says that you'd give a man hell, hot all th' time and givin' him your tongue when you wasn't happy about somethin'. He says it ain't a woman's right to drive a man when he don't want to be driven."

"He's right," Martha said. "Only I wouldn't have that kind of a man." She dropped her hand lightly to Emma's shoulder. "We'd best get inside. Brazos says the Comanches like to wander around at night."

Martha bolted the heavy door. The fire in the hearth had died to a bed of cherry-red coals and she lighted the candles. A yellow glow chased the darkness back.

Earlier in the day they had made candles and now these were ready to be taken out of the tapered molds. Candlemaking was every woman's chore unless her husband could afford an oil lamp. The candles were long and thick, almost two inches at the base. Martha rinsed the molds in hot water and the tallow next to the metal melted, letting the candles slip out easily.

With a winter's supply of candles put away, the two women settled themselves to the endless task of sewing. Because Brazos had an eye for small details, there was a stock of needles and thread. Martha had saved several muskrat pelts and was stitching them into a warm, pullover jacket with a hood at the top. Emma worked on a new pair of slippers for Martin, driving the saddlemaker's awl through the heavy soles for the waxed stitching.

They worked for an hour without conversation. Once Emma rose to throw more wood on the fire. When she sat down again she said, "I got no right to be askin', but did Brazos promise you pretties when you marry him?"

"No," Martha said evenly. "I don't want pretties anyway. Just him." She regarded Emma with such soberness that the girl grew uncomfortable. "You don't love Martin now, do you?"

"I married him," Emma stated. The candlelight danced on her smooth skin and made her eyes seem darker. "Ain't that sayin' enough?"

"Not enough to be happy," she said.

"I—I better get some more wood for the fire," Emma said and went to the door, sliding the bar back. She glanced at Martha and found the young woman's calm eyes on her, and her nervousness increased.

"Better take the rifle," Martha said and Emma opened the door. The breeze fanned the candle flame and the light dimmed, but there was enough to outline the tall figure of a man in the doorway.

Her scream tore through the silence like a gunshot and Martha's chair toppled as she lunged for the rifle. The man stood there, wrapped in shadows, and when Martha snatched up the gun, he shoved the door aside, shouting, "Whoa there! Whoa !"

The door slammed shut and the candle steadied, revealing Ray Olroyd.

"Damn you anyway!" Martha snapped, her hands shaking. She let the rifle down to half cock. "Ain't you got better sense? Where you been, Ray? You've been gone ten days."

"Here and there," Ray said smoothly and moved into the room. He set his rifle and jug of whiskey on the table, then gave Emma a sidling glance. "Didn't mean to give you a scare, Emma. You know I wouldn't hurt you none."

"What do you want here, Ray?" Martha asked curtly.

She still held Brazos' rifle and now laid it on the table by the pelts. She studied her brother. Olroyd had a shaggy, untrimmed beard, and from the dirt on his clothes he had been traveling.

"Just come around to see if you was all right," he said. "Hell, I been gone and I wanted to see you. You'd think a brother didn't give a damn." He paused to stroke his face. "Can't say's I'm rightly pleased, your bein' here without Caine speakin' the words to marry you and all." He smiled and a dull light came into his eyes. "If Caine changed his wind, you might have trouble findin' a man. None of *us* is fool enough to think you went home *every* night."

"That's enough from you!" Martha said sharply. "You've said your howdys so turn around and light out of here."

"I didn't mean nothin'," Olroyd said, looking at Emma. "Sure ain't seen much of you since you took up with Martin. Figured you'd drop over and jaw with Ma, but I guess Martin's laid the law down, ain't he?"

"You and me's got nothin' to talk about," Emma said. "I told you that the last time."

"Well," Ray said, "I sure didn't come here to be unpleasant." He hooked his finger in the handle of the jug and pulled the corncob. "Sure you ladies wouldn't like a snort? It grows hair." Finally he shrugged and upended it, gurgling noisily. He lowered the jug and turned his head sharply as a man's voice called out from the flats. A fleeting nervousness crossed his face and when he went to pick up his rifle, Martha kicked it clattering to the floor. Ray cursed under his breath and bent to pick it up, stiffening when Martha raised Brazos' gun to nudge him in the chest with the muzzle.

"Just leave it lay," she said flatly.

125

"Maybe that's Martin comin' back," Emma said hopefully.

"Martin ain't comin' back," Olroyd said and Martha gave him a sharp glance. Olroyd moved away from the rifle she held and stood by the wall where the shadows were thickest. The man called out again, closer this time.

Emma opened her mouth to speak, for she recognized the voice, but Martha's look silenced her. "Don't open the door," Martha said, the rifle pointed at the panel. "If he pushes once without knocking, I'll blow a hole through him."

"Jesus Christ," Ray muttered. "That's a hell of a way to meet a man."

"I didn't ask you to bring anyone here," she said as the man's knuckles rattled against the door.

"Hey in there! It's me—Asa McClintock! Open the damn door!"

"Open it," Martha said and Emma slid back the bolt.

Entering, Asa grinned and blinked against the candlelight. Then his grin faded as he saw Martha holding the rifle. "What the hell," he said. "You got no call to point that at me."

He caught a glimpse of Olroyd standing in the deep shadows and jumped back, startled. Olroyd laughed softly. "Give you a worry, didn't it?" He shifted his jug from one arm to the other. "You knew it couldn't be, but it still scared you, didn't it?"

"I wasn't scared," Asa said. His long face turned crafty. "I'm through worryin' about that." He looked at Emma. "I'm payin' a call to my own sister. Let anyone make somethin' out of that."

"That's what I say," Olroyd said and offered the jug. "Better have a snort. That long walk must have got your heat up."

"It sure did," he said and made a point not to look at Martha. He took his drink and handed the jug back. Asa also showed signs of travel, Martha noticed. He was dirty and his clothes were dust-stained. His face sported another inch of hair and his eyes were large and very bright. They watered continually.

"Sure is lonesome country with all the pretty girls married off or fixin' to," Olroyd said, taking another drink.

"Sure is," Asa echoed. He looked boldly at Martha's full figure and pulled his glance away when he could no longer stand the unfriendliness in her eyes. "Purely drives a man to desperation," he said, laughing softly. "Why, the other day I caught myself lookin' them Ryker girls up and down."

"Where have you two been?" Martha asked. "You ain't been around the settlement."

Asa waved his hand toward the mountains. "Trappin'. Can't let Brazos make it all, now can we?"

"You don't know nothin' about trappin'," Martha said. "What have you been up to?"

"Have another drink," Olroyd suggested and offered Asa the jug. Asa reached for it and Martha stepped around the table, sending it to the floor with one sweep of the rifle barrel.

"God damn!" Ray shouted. "What the hell did you do that for?" He stared at the broken pieces and the clear liquid soaking onto the bare floor.

The coffee pot began thumping and the room filled with the strong flavor. Asa sniffed and said, "They must have known he was comin', they got coffee on."

"I'll have to get some more water," Emma said and picked up the bucket. She moved past and behind Ray

127

Olroyd.

"I better go with you," Ray said. "Don't want some Injun liftin' that pretty hair of yours."

"You stay where you're at!" Martha ordered. "She can get water by herself."

Olroyd laughed and took a backward step toward the door. Martha shifted the rifle until it covered him. "I mean it, Ray! Let her be!"

"What's got into you?" he asked innocently. When Martha continued to stare, he looked at Asa. "Don't this beat hell, though?" Asa looked as though he thought it did and this gave Olroyd encouragement. He pointed to his sister. "You wouldn't shoot me, would you, Martha?" He took another sidling step toward the door and prodded Emma behind him with his elbow.

"What'll I do?" Emma asked in a small voice.

"Will you really shoot me, Martha? I ain't done nothin'." He shot a glance at Asa McClintock. "Asa's standin' there, waitin' to pay his howdy, and you ain't even noticed him. Has she, Asa?"

"She surely ain't," McClintock said and Martha switched her eyes to him. Olroyd was waiting for this and he shoved against Emma, throwing open the door and driving her outside. He slammed the door before Martha could stop him.

She started around the table, but Asa's voice stopped her. "Now don't you fret about her, Martha. I don't guess Ray means to hurt her none."

"You dirty pig!" Martha snapped. "Just because she's dumb, you got to take advantage of her! If he touches her, Martin will cut his heart out."

She bent and picked up Olroyd's rifle, cocking it before laying it on the table, the muzzle pointed at Asa's stomach.

128

He licked his lips and pointed to it, saying, "I would surely appreciate you takin' that thing away from me. Makes me nervous, cocked that way."

"Let me hear one yell out there," Martha said softly, "and I'll blow a hole through you, then shoot Ray with my own gun."

"Well now," Asa said, his Adam's apple bobbing, "I surely wouldn't want to see that happen." He turned his head toward the door and yelled, "Damn it now, Ray, you be gentle with her, you hear?"

There was no answering sound, and in the silence a log settled in the fireplace. Finally there came a mild scuffling and then someone struck a blow. Martha smiled thinly when Ray yelped and cursed as Emma hit him with the wooden bucket; the thump was unmistakable. Asa shifted his big feet and made a vague motion with his hands. "Seems to me you're gettin' damn pure of a sudden. A man don't need no wishin' stick to figure out what a good job you done takin' care of Brazos Caine."

"Get out of here," Martha said. "When Brazos comes back I'll tell him you called. Likely he'll be over to see you about it."

"Wait a minute now," McClintock said, suddenly cautious. "You'n me's done our share of spoonin'. Sure, I never put you in no fine house like he done, but there's no call to be forgettin'." He smiled weakly. "I wouldn't wait for Brazos, Martha, 'cause he's liable not to be comin' back."

He took a step toward the table. In the yard, Ray yelped again and there was the soft sound of a struggle. Cloth ripped suddenly and Asa took another step as Martha's hand fell to the gun lock. He divined that she was going to shoot and tried to close the gap. The rifle blasted and he halted suddenly, his mouth flying open with shock. The recoil tore the rifle off the table, sending it clattering to the floor. McClintock sat down suddenly, both hands clasped across his stomach.

The room was hazy with powder smoke and the odor made her eyes water. Ray Olroyd cursed and he flung the door open. Martha raised Brazos' rifle as he framed himself in the opening. He stared goggle-eyed at McClintock who coughed blood.

"Jesus God! What the hell you done?"

"Shot a dirty dog," Martha said. "What did he mean, Brazos ain't comin' back? What you been up to?"

"Jesus," Olroyd repeated, his eyes held by McClintock's convulsions. He tore his eyes away and looked at his sister, then launched himself in a dive that carried him clear of the door. She fired. Splinters flaked away from the upright and the bullet whined away in the night. Olroyd was running across the yard.

In the following silence, Martha went to the mantel and calmly loaded Brazos' rifle. McClintock groaned softly on the floor and thrashed his legs jerkily. Martha did not look at him. She went outside to find Emma.

By the well curbing Emma knelt in the dirt, the upper half of her dress in shreds around her waist. The faint light gleamed on her shoulders and breasts and Martha put her hands beneath her arms and lifted her.

"I shot your brother," she said. "I think he's dying."

Martha raised her head as a halloo sounded from across the flats and a square of light shot from Jubal Caine's doorway. Martha pulled at Emma, trying to get her back inside. Emma came out of her trance and said, "He didn't hurt me none. Nobody can hurt me any more."

She stepped past Martha and went inside. Martha left

the door open and watched Emma as she went to the bed and sat down, unmindful of her near-nakedness.

"Put the blanket over you," Martha said. "Jubal Caine will be here pretty soon."

Placing the rifle on the table, she forced herself to kneel by Asa McClintock. The man's eyes were open and glazed with pain. She said, "I'm sorry, Asa, but you were always the kind who never believed anyone else."

"I—hit bad," he said and sweat ran down his whiskered face. He moved his hand and touched his stomach. "Spine—I think." He tried to strike her in the face. "Damn little—whore."

Jubal Caine's moccasins made no sound as he came across the yard at a dead run. He halted upon entering and when he saw Asa, pushed Martha aside to kneel. McClintock's eyes were staring vacantly and a dull film was beginning to form over them.

Jubal Caine stood up slowly and looked around. "You do this?"

"I warned him," Martha said, "but he's a McClintock and you can't tell 'em anythin'." She scrubbed a hand across her forehead and started to tremble. Caine walked to the door and closed it, sliding the bar in place. He glanced at Emma sitting on the bed with the quilt around her, but said nothing about it.

"That other shot? You fire that too?"

She nodded. "At Ray. I meant to kill him too." She looked sharply at Jubal Caine. "Asa said that Brazos ain't comin' back. You know what that means?"

"No," he admitted and brushed his whiskers. "Where's Ray been? Not around the settlement since Brazos pantsed him that night." He shook his head. "I don't know what he meant, unless he's been up to some devilment, him and Asa."

131

"Can—can you take him out of here?" she asked.

He grunted and said, "I'll see that he's taken home. Expect Jeb'll be over in th' mornin', but I'll be here first thing."

He opened the door and came back, lifting Asa. Martha closed and barred the door after he went out.

From the bed, Emma said, "He kept grabbin' at me. He tore my dress."

"We'll get you a new dress," Martha said and sat down at the table, her hands flat to still the trembling. She studied Emma. The girl sat motionless, her eyes staring and vacant. Martha got up from the table and crossed to her. "Emma, are you all right?"

When the girl didn't answer, Martha whipped her hand across Emma's face. For a moment the girl was stunned, the white imprint of Martha's hand bold on her cheek, then she tipped her head forward and her shoulders began to shake. Tears fell on her hands.

At the fireplace, Martha jabbed viciously at the halfburned logs. "Goddamn men anyway," she said and stared at the leaping flames. Emma stopped crying at last and a deep silence moved into the room.

CHAPTER THIRTEEN

WAKING WITH THE FIRST TINGE OF DAWN, BRAZOS Caine left Captain Travers' quarters and walked across the parade to the long building serving as the enlisted men's mess. He had his corn-meal mush, bacon and scalding coffee, then recrossed the parade. Martin was waiting outside the main gate.

The dawn light grew brighter and distant objects came more clearly into focus. The Sergeant-Major was forming three troops by the barracks and the duty sergeant called the role while the officer-of-the-day strutted past, saber clanking against his leg. The first edge of the sun appeared as Brazos went to the mover's camp. Bold light shot slanting rays across the land and clouds stood out like suspended balls of cotton.

Going to Modry's fire, Brazos found most of the men gathered there. He said, "Had a word with army scouts this mornin' at mess. The Apaches are out again, but I've a feelin' we can get through." He turned his head as Martin came up and stood against a wagon wheel, his bruised face sullen. "Better get the wagons lined out," he told Modry. "I'll join you with my ox carts within a mile." He glanced at Martin. "You goin' to scout or play lone wolf again?"

"I'll go along," Martin said, touching the spot where Brazos had hit him. "I want to stay close to you, Brazos. We got some settlin' up to do later."

"Suit yourself," Brazos said and went back to the palisade for his carts. He yoked the oxen, tied them in a string and left the fort at a plodding pace.

Seven wagons were stretched in a ragged line, waiting. Seven families and seven different dreams, he decided. The men sat on the high seats, patiently waiting for the signal to move. From beneath the gray canvas tops, children peered out and the women sat beside their men, hands folded in their laps as patiently as rocks enduring the wearing effect of time.

Pausing by Modry's off wheel, Brazos said, "I'll lead with my carts. Be a long haul. Ten-twelve days. You got some young men in your party, Modry. I'd be obliged if they'd tend my oxen. Give me a chance to scout with Martin."

"I'll see that it's done," Modry promised and Brazos

took a point three hundred yards distance. Martin waited there and when Brazos came up, they turned, striking out toward the hills. Behind them, the wagons strung out like a disjointed serpent. Heavy wheels ground the earth and a shaft of dust rose slowly, thickening until it was a tan cloud partially obscuring the sun.

"Talk about smoke signals," Martin said and trotted away, disappearing over a slight rise of land.

Through the morning they moved toward the mountains, beginning the climb that led to the faint, rutted trail hanging against massive walls. All movement was slow, a mile-an-hour pace at best. The trail grew increasingly difficult for Modry's four-wheeled wagons. The Mexican carts rode the chopped land with little difficulty, but the wagons were jolted unmercifully. The rumble of the wagons was a continuous pound as wheels struck rocks and rain-washed ruts. Wagon boxes twisted to the contours of the tortured trail, emitting a new set of groans. The clank of drag-chains increased; whips cracked steadily like the distant popping of small arms. The dust rose thicker and hovered like a cloud of low smoke, marking their progress as they climbed ever higher.

Toward evening they passed the first sharp uplift of the mountains and were deep in this wild land. Twice during the afternoon Brazos Caine had caught the bright mirror flashes of the Apaches signaling each other with polished silver discs.

For a camp site, he chose a level plateau and formed the wagons in a tight circle. His own carts were placed within the small area and Modry complained about it. "Tight as you've drawn us, there's hardly room to move around."

"You won't need to move much," Brazos said. "You

134

see them mirror flashes this afternoon?"

"Yes. I've been meanin' to ask about it."

"Apaches send messages that way." Brazos said. "There's more'n one band of hostiles in these hills. We'll use a four-man guard tonight." He turned as Martin's soft footfall drew near. "You see anything out there?"

"'Paches? You never see 'em," he said and squatted, his rifle across his knees.

"About those Apaches," Modry said. The big man's voice was concerned. "I wouldn't want to put the women in any danger if I could help it."

"There's no place around here free of danger," Brazos said. "Ain't many men who know 'Paches. I speak a little Coyotero but on the whole they ain't the kind of Indian a man gets acquainted with easy."

"We mean them no harm," Modry said. "Surely they can understand that, can't they?"

"Every man means harm to an Apache," Brazos said dryly. "They're a dyin' race, Modry; a lot of their women are barren. From the day an Apache can walk, he's taught to kill or be killed. The games they play ain't the kind your younguns play. They take a boy and place him out in the open so they can pelt him with stones. He ducks as many as he can but when he gets hurt, he don't dare cry about it."

"Damned savages!" Modry said.

"You're wrong there," Brazos said. "Of all the Indians I ever seen, I'll take the Apache over any other. Cruel, yes. A fighter? Guess he's the best. Brave? Apaches have no word for it but their words are not like ours, meanin' only one thing. Their word means that their body is strong like a tree. 'His heart is like a bear's, who will fight to his last breath.' It means that

135

all fear has been driven from the Apache heart and he looks on death as sort of a reward." He paused to stare off into the dusk. "Their words mean a lot of things. They paint the color of the sunsets and the smell of the desert in bloom."

"You ought to be a goddamned preacher," Martin said. "You got the wind for it." With the sun melted behind the hills, the sky turned a muddy gray.

"We fought Comanches from Mission San Angelo on," Modry said. "Lost some good men." He looked at his camp through the crowding darkness. "Can we have fires?"

"Why not?" Martin said. "They know we're here."

Modry passed the word and fires were lighted around the inner perimeter. Brazos watched these for a while, then turned away. Scaling the sloping sides of the trail, Brazos and Martin took a place two hundred yards above the camp. They settled among the rocks, commanding a clear view. The cook fires were cores of brightness and they threw shadows like ink splashes against the canvas wagon tops.

Martin and Brazos did not speak. Martin laid down his rifle and produced jerky from his possible sack.

The night grew older. Above them, a small rock dislodged and came tumbling down, gathering other loose rock with it. Brazos turned and listened with his head cocked sharply to one side.

In the camp below, voices came across the distance and the fires were bright tongues of light. Brazos and Martin were dark shapes huddled in the blackest shadows. Overhead, clouds partially obscured the moon and only a faint light washed the blackness to a slightly lighter shade.

There was no sound above them now and Martin held

up three fingers. Brazos nodded and waited. Within an hour, the fires began to die out in the camp as the movers settled for the night. Touching Martin, Brazos left the sheltering rocks and together they edged their way carefully off the slope to the parked wagons.

He drew Martin close and said softly, "Something's wrong here. There's three of 'em and they're movin' in, but where are the others?"

They ran the rest of the way bent over, shielded from the revealing lightness of the skyline. A few minutes later they slipped between two wagons and a man grunted in surprise, his rifle raised.

Brazos spoke softly. "Three Apaches are workin' their way off the hillside. Keep a sharp lookout, but I doubt if you'll see 'em in time to do any good."

The man swallowed hard. "I don't want a knife in me."

"I don't think they mean to fight," Brazos said. He touched Martin and added, "These men are ready to jump out of their hides. Keep an eye on 'em and I'll scout the camp."

"Ummm," Martin grunted and moved toward the three guards on the other side of the camp. The fires were nearly dead—only red embers marked them. The wagons were dark shapes and Brazos divided his attention between the guards and Martin, who moved carefully around the inner perimeter.

Martin put light wood on several fires, causing the flames to shoot skyward. The wagons were outlined more clearly. Brazos crouched by the dropped tongue of one wagon, listening for the familiar night sounds and found them absent. He turned to observe Martin and his back was to the outer ring. Slowly, his nostrils distended and he felt the hair on the back of his neck rise. The musk odor of animal scent was strong and he whirled quickly, his hand slapping the bone butt of his Colt's pistol.

The shock of seeing the Apaches standing within touching distance was like a saber thrust. Firelight glinted on their naked chests and the dark eyes glowed savagely as they watched Brazos and the guard. The guard, warned by Brazos' movement, brought up his rifle, but Brazos batted it aside.

"What the goddamned hell!" the man stormed.

"Look at their faces," Brazos said. "No paint. Apaches won't fight without paint."

The guard turned his head and yelled, and the camp came alive. Women yelled and children added their excited cries to the men's shouts of alarm. Almost instantly Martin was at Brazos' side, and Brazos said softly, "Don't point your gun at them, friend." The movers assembled, armed and ready to kill. When the Apaches stepped over the dropped tongue, Brazos said, "Get those fools back, Martin, before they start something."

Martin used his voice like a club, driving them back. The men lowered their rifles and Brazos spoke to the Apaches. *"Seekist."*

The Apache answered briefly and then Brazos spoke again, a mixture of Coyotero and Spanish. The Apache's face showed no change in expression while he listened. When he spoke, he gestured with his hands.

They were tall men, and well proportioned. From the waist down they wore breechclouts and wraparound leggings. Loose cloth shirts, silver arm bands and a bright sash around the waist completed their dress. Colored headbands kept their long hair away from their faces.

The Apache spoke again and Brazos listened. He turned to Modry and said, "Says he's in trouble. They had a brush with Comanches and only a few remain of their band."

"What do they expect us to do?" Modry asked. The Apaches were alien to him and he distrusted them.

"Get some food for 'em," he said and spoke again to the Apache. Modry barked an order to his wife and she set a large kettle on the fire, stirring the coals to a new heat.

Martin came close to Brazos and said, "You believe him?"

"Don't you?"

"I like dead Indians," he said softly. "Find out how many's left. Maybe we can handle 'em."

Brazos locked eyes with the mountain man and said, "Not this time, Martin. You break my word and I'll kill you."

Martin glowered and fingered his rifle, then wheeled and squatted by the wheel of a wagon. Modry shifted his feet and Brazos spoke again to the Apache.

"His name is Tuscos; I've heard of him. He says that he recognized me and knew I fought Comanches and Mexicans. You got any tobacco, Modry? . . . then give him some."

The tobacco passed back and forth and when the Apaches had the chew softened, Brazos talked at greater length with Tuscos.

"He says there's eight left in his band. The others were killed when they walked into a Comanche ambush twenty miles up the trail. Better get the women and kids into the wagons, Modry. The men can go about their business. It makes the Apaches nervous to have people standin' around."

"I don't trust 'em," Modry said.

"Man," Brazos chided, "they didn't have to come in like this, friendly like. They could have killed you just as easy. If Tuscos gives his word, he'll die before he breaks it. Tuscos says he speaks of peace with his heart in his hand. Better do as I say and hurry that grub along."

Grumbling, Modry turned and Brazos squatted, inviting Tuscos and the others to do likewise. Brazos took the stew pot from the spot Mrs. Modry left it—she would come no closer than twenty feet—and offered it to Tuscos. They ate quickly and afterward wiped their greasy hands on their arms. One Apache took the kettle with what was left of the stew and disappeared. Tuscos spoke again and Brazos listened attentively. He turned his head and shot a quick look in Martin's direction. The mountain man was standing. He came over.

"What the hell was that he said?"

"Tuscos claims Esqueda's Comanches did this to his people. He says the ambush was intended for us and that he got caught in it instead."

Martin made a disgusted noise. "I heard that. What was that other? I didn't catch it all," Brazos hesitated and Martin hit him on the arm. "Come on, come on— what'd he say?"

"Tuscos claims he knows where Esqueda's place is."

"Jesus!" Martin said and slapped his thigh. He tried to speak to Tuscos, but his Apache was too limited. Finally he turned to Brazos. "Ask him how to get there." When Brazos hesitated, Martin's voice dropped to a rumble. "Damn you, I said, ask him!"

Brazos spoke again and the Apache listened intently. When he answered, he glanced often at Martin and Martin squirmed, impatient for an answer. Finally

140

Brazos said, "He claims that Esqueda moved after the white man—meanin' Clay—was killed 'cause he knew you'd be after him. He won't say where the place is, Martin. He wants to make' a deal. We got to go with him on the raid."

"Tell him we'll go!"

Brazos shook his head. "We got to think of the settlement. Gettin' a road through and trade built up is more important than killin' Esqueda."

"Not to me," Martin said flatly. "You think I traipsed all over the country with you because I liked your company? I kept hopin' I'd meet that Mex or someone who knew where to find him. You ain't goin' to have no peace until he's dead and you know it. You don't come with me, then I'll go alone."

"I got to talk it over with the settlement," Brazos said. "Martin, I'm thinkin' of somebody beside myself."

"That's your own fool fault," Martin said. "All right, I'll make *you* a deal. Promise Tuscos you'll go along. We'll take the goods into Ryker's and then leave. You'll be doin' your damned duty as you call it and I'll get Esqueda's ears."

Brazos considered it, then spoke to Tuscos. Martin sat back now, no longer paying attention. His hands moved over the slick buckskin covering his thighs and his thoughts were dark. The movers were in their wagons and there was no movement around the camp. The two Apaches came back with the empty stew pot and lay on the ground, soon asleep. Brazos and Tuscos sat crosslegged and talked in low tones. A deep silence settled over the land and the fires died, one by one, while Apache and white man sealed a bargain.

The next day the land grew increasingly rough and

141

traveling became agony. The pace was slowed even further and the men dismounted to walk beside their ox teams, long whips cracking, urging the animals on to greater efforts.

They were working through a mountain pass, traveling along a shelf of rock barely wide enough to accommodate the iron-bound wheels. The Apaches acted as outriders while Martin worked the point.

Brazos kept thinking of the fight that had cost Tuscos his strength. There was no doubt in his mind that the Comanches had been waiting for the movers. It was no blind raiding party, Brazos was sure of this. The Comanches had known beforehand what they were coming here for and he wondered how they got this information.

The movers did not like Tuscos and the Apaches. Modry spoke of it. "Wish them Indians'd get the hell out of here. Makes the women jumpy."

"Sure they don't make *you* jumpy?" Brazos grinned when Modry flushed guiltily. He took a pull at his canteen and added, "I guess they don't like us either, but they'll cotton to us if it will get 'em somethin'. Tuscos' band wasn't big to start with; maybe twenty in all. Apaches don't like other Indians, Modry. They gather in small bands and roam."

"This Tuscos must think a heap of you, comin' in like he did."

Brazos smiled. "I've been in his Apacheria and he ain't never caught me. To Tuscos, that means I'm as good as he is." He took another swig from his canteen and corked it. "Trouble with Apaches is that they got no land like other Indians. They don't plant nothin', just steal. An Apache'll ride a horse to death, then steal another one. Mexicans hate 'em for runnin' off with

142

their women. That's how come Apaches speak Spanish; half their women is Mex."

He left Modry and the train and moved on up the trail. Toward evening he paused on a high rock and looked back. The wagons had halted and there was a large group of men gathered around one wagon. He left his perch and ran back to see what the trouble was.

The men were talking among themselves, passing suggestions back and forth, when he pushed his way through. One of the wheels had shed a rim, the dust and heat having shrunk the wood while the pounding over rocks had expanded the rim.

"Get the wagon wheel off," he said and men unhitched, using the heavy tongue for a peavy. Rocks were placed beneath the axle and the bed elevated. Two men wrestled the heavy wheel and laid it on the ground. "There's a creek a mile or so down the canyon," Brazos said. "Modry, get five men on this wheel and we'll put the rim back on." He hefted the fifty-pound rim and started off down the steep sidehill. Modry and five cursing men followed him, fighting the heavy wheel all the way.

Because he moved faster, Brazos had a fire started and the rim buried in the flames by the time Modry and the sweating men got the wheel down to the creek bed. The trail was a thousand feet above them and the wagons were invisible from this point.

Brazos ordered the wheel dumped into the creek to soak, causing it to swell. While the rim heated, Brazos cut two long poles. With a mars on each end, the red-hot rim could be lifted from the fire and carried. The wheel was removed from the water, and Brazos ordered the hot rim lifted. He pounded this over the wheel with a rock and then the wheel and rim were immersed again. Steam rose in a cloud and the water rumbled. After twenty minutes, it was removed, the rim tightly shrunk onto the swollen wheel.

"Take it back up," Brazos said. "Pass the word around, Modry, to soak loose spokes with wet rags."

A stout pole was cut, inserted through the hub, and the wheel was worked back to the road. By the time the wheel had been replaced, a gentle dusk was falling. From higher ground, an Apache came down and spoke to Brazos, then was gone again.

"Stay here," Brazos said, "but start no fires."

He trotted on ahead and, twenty minutes later, met Tuscos on high ground commanding a sweep of the gorge they must pass through.

"Here," Tuscos said, "my braves die." A slight smile came into his eyes. "But Comanche die here too."

Brazos worked his way around the rocky ledge. In the failing light he examined the ground, catching sight of occasional scuff marks. No moccasin made these, he told himself, and continued his search. In the level spots, dirt had been washed down to make a fill and he found other tracks. Finally he squatted behind a huge boulder and turned the situation over in his mind. He brushed the dirt into small piles with his hands, lifting it and letting it sift through his fingers. Several times he did this, then stopped and stared at his palm. Caught between his fingers was a brass percussion cap, fired and split on both sides, but it was too small to be a rifle cap. It fit a Colt's pistol!

The full implication struck Brazos like a blow in the face. A white man had led the Comanches here! A man from the settlement, for there were no others who knew he was going to Fort Davis. There was no other conclusion to be drawn.

Someone from Ryker's was in league with the

CHAPTER FOURTEEN

WHEN BRAZOS RETURNED TO THE WAGONS, HE DID not tell Martin of his discovery. Mentally, he tallied up the number of Colt's pistols in the settlement. His father had one. So did Martin. Ray Olroyd had a .28 caliber which used a very small cap. The cap he had found would have fit his own pistols which were .36 caliber. Then there were the two pistols he had given to Jeb McClintock. But Brazos could not remember whether Jeb had come back for them or not. The last he had seen of them, they were on Ryker's shelf.

Modry wanted to remain here for the night, but Brazos insisted that they go on. Ahead lay the gorge, a perfect ambush, and he wanted to get through there while he knew it was clear. Tuscos and five of his men went ahead and scouted the wagons through.

Nine miles on the other side the dawn slipped over the hills and Brazos selected a camp site where the land tapered into a shallow run. The place was relatively open and he ordered the wagons circled. The men were grumbling about a night without sleep and Brazos had Modry pass the word that they would remain here until noon, then push on. Martin showed no inclination to take the scout and Brazos went over to a wagon where Martin sought shade. Brazos intended to discuss this.

"What's the matter up there, Martin?"

"Too many Indians," Martin said. He lay with his parfleche for a pillow, his stocky arms behind his head.

"Can't you get along with anybody?" Brazos asked. He hunkered down to shield himself from the blazing

145

sunlight.

Martin's eyes contained a dark anger. "Maybe I'm tired of gettin' along. Tired of takin' orders from you."

"Then get out of camp," Brazos said flatly.

"I'm sick of your bull," Martin said, rolling over. "Time's come to get shed of it once and for all." He crawled from beneath the wagon and stood up. Brazos came to his feet and waited. Martin's pistol and rifle were beneath the wagon, but he had his knife. He touched it. "Was I to draw this, I'd kill you, Brazos. I don't fool with man or beast."

"Why you always got to be fightin' somethin'?" Brazos asked. "Seems that when you're wrong and get called for it, the only answer you got is to fight."

"You scared to meet me? Is that it?" Martin's knuckles were white, so tightly did he grip the knife handle. But he did not draw it.

"I offered to fight you once—" Brazos began, then turned as one of Tuscos' Apaches came pumping over a small rise. He ran swiftly, leaping over rocks and small slashes. Brazos left Martin and went to meet him.

The Apache stopped and began to talk rapidly, then Brazos ran back to the wagons. Martin had forgotten his anger. "Trouble?"

Modry and several others began to gather around the wagon. "There's Comanches over the next hogback," Brazos said. "'Bout three miles, Tuscos says. They're the ones who laid the ambush for us." He looked the terrain over again. Had he a choice he would not have picked this place, for the sloping hills on both sides gave the enemy the advantage. But he had no time now, so he gave Modry his orders. "Drive the wagons in a string. Tell the women and kids to stay under cover."

"Dammit, man," Modry said testily, "we need level

146

ground to fight on and there's nothing here but hills."

"This'll have to do," Brazos told him and glanced at Martin. "You still want to fight?" .

"I'll kill an Indian any time," he said and got his weapons. Modry began to organize his movers, while on the hillside Tuscos appeared with his warriors, preparing an ambush of his own. The men in the train were deploying along the ground, protected by the heavy wheels. Powder, shot and caps were laid out and each man looked nervously at his neighbor.

Brazos walked up and down the line of wagons, giving advice, helping ease the strain of waiting. *That's the trouble with fighting Indians, he thought. The waitin's worse than the attack.*

Drawing Modry aside, he said, "They'll have to come over that swale. Tell your men to aim careful and save their firepower. The Comanches have a way of fightin' that's damned dangerous. They'll send in th' first wave to make you shoot, then before you can poke a new charge down the barrel, the second wave'll hit you and it's all over."

"That ain't very comfortin'," Modry said.

"You got twelve men here," Brazos said, "countin' the older boys. Let three come with us. We got revolvin' pistols and we'll bait a trap for them Comanches."

Modry singled out the three Scovill boys. They came over, their long rifles cradled in their arms. Brazos explained what he had in mind and led them into the rocky ground a dozen yards to the side of the wagons. He settled them into good shelter and saw that he was between the Apaches and the wagons.

The Apaches were making hand signals.

Martin edged up, squatted and said, "What's that bastard wavin' for?"

147

Brazos shot him an irritated glance, but said nothing. He glanced at the Scovill boys. The oldest was not ready to shave, but he seemed undisturbed by the fact that he would soon be fighting for his life. They sat with their eyes riveted to the crest of the swale, their long rifles ready.

"Shoot after we start shootin'," Brazos told them.

"Why shore," the oldest one said.

Martin laid out his pistol and checked the charges in his revolving rifle. He glanced at Brazos. "You mad at me?"

"I'm nothing at you," Brazos said softly. "Shut up and leave me alone."

For ten minutes there was no sound, then a Comanche topped the ridge and saw the parked wagons. He eased back out of sight.

"Christ," one of the Scovill boys said, "Is that what we're fightin' ? He's pretty runty."

"He can fight, sonny," Brazos said. "Just see that you can."

The brothers squirmed to more comfortable positions, the barrels of their rifles outthrust among the rocks. Brazos listened and knew that the Comanches were massing on the other side of the hill.

He drew his pistols and held them cocked in his hands. In his mind's eye he could see them gathering. How strong, he didn't know, but they would be in a line awaiting the signal to charge.

Suddenly the noonday quiet was ruptured by shrill yells and the rolling thunder of racing ponies. The Comanches broke off the hill and started down, their skidding horses forming a ragged line. The sight was breathtaking, the warriors painted and streaming feathers from their war bonnets. Lances were decorated brightly and sported the hair of many enemies.

Several men lying beneath the wagons commenced firing although the range was over four hundred yards. Brazos knew what conclusions the Comanches would draw from this. Only fools wasted powder. On they came, a cloud of dust rising to stream out behind them. From the wagons, several more shots rang out, the bullets falling short of the oncoming line. From beneath the wagon beds, puffs of powder smoke wafted up and away but not one pony stumbled or spilled its rider.

The Comanches veered slightly and closed the range to two hundred yards. More shots burst from beneath the wagons, a ragged volley that had no effect. Brazos said, "Goddamn that Modry! Can't he tell the range is too long?"

The men who had fired hastily pounded home powder and shot; the Comanches raced on toward the line of wagons. Someone else fired, a cool shot at two hundred yards, and a brave reeled drunkenly on his horse, finally falling off.

With a hundred yards separating the Comanches from the wagons, they passed the hiding place of Tuscos and his braves. The Apaches scudded out and fell in behind the attackers, notching arrows to their bows. The movers were firing more effectively now since the Comanches were within easy range, but the shooting was still spasmodic and without direction. Brazos waited until the Comanches dropped to a level below him, then raised his hand. The small party fired a withering volley that searched the painted ranks. It wiped ponies clean and Tuscos released his flight of arrows, causing complete panic among the Comanches. They were confused and shocked by this new danger. Martin was firing his eight-shot rifle with cool

149

precision, giving the Scovill boys a chance to reload.

The Comanche charge had been broken and the warriors wheeled their ponies in chopped circles. Modry rallied with a withering fire. The Comanche leader fell and the others plunged in wild retreat, the rising dust obscuring them.

Tuscos and his braves raced from boulder to boulder, entering the fray with lance and knife. Horses were hamstrung and riders unseated. Brazos ordered firing suspended, for friend and foe were engulfed in a cloud of dust. For several minutes the battle raged, then the Comanches broke away in a shattered group and made for the ridge. Modry began firing again, the booming racket of rifles laying a sharp sound over the valley. The range was too great for effect and the firing stopped as the last of the Comanches disappeared over the top.

Powder smoke and dust rose in a fat cloud, even though the battle was over. A fickle wind caught it and washed it away. Tuscos and his braves assembled, but their ranks were thinner by three. In the wagons, Modry took a hasty count and found Summers dying. The dead Comanches were strewn along the path of attack. Brazos led his party out of the rocks.

One of the Scovill boys had a wound in his arm and handed his rifle to his brother while he bandaged it. Modry had completed his check by the time Brazos arrived. The women were emerging from the wagons, wide-eyed and frightened, calling to their men.

Besides Summers, four more had been wounded, one seriously. Summers would not live out the hour. Looking around at the shocked faces, Brazos said, "Better get your people ready to move."

Modry said, "Man, I've a man dyin'. Can't we wait to bury him?"

"If he ain't dead and buried in an hour," Brazos said, reloading his pistols, "we're movin' on." He glanced at Modry and found the man's eyes hot and rebellious. "Look," Brazos said, "this country ain't safe to moon around in. You got an hour like I told you."

"There's no Christian feeling left," Modry said and walked wearily away.

Summers died and three men carried him to the side of the trail and made a rock cairn over him. A woman began to wail loudly.

Martin walked away and sat down, his back to the group. Brazos turned when Tuscos came up. There was no change in the Apache's expression save a new pleasure in his dark eyes. He spoke quietly in Coyotero. "Sun-in-the-Hair is a brother. He thinks like an Apache chief, in terms of the ambush."

"Apaches are wise," Brazos said. "With a few men, they defeat great numbers. I have learned from the Apaches."

"And I have watched," Tuscos said, the light deepening in his eyes. "Several times I have supplied the lessons. Many times Sun-in-the-Hair has come into Tuscos' Apacheria, but has never been caught." His eyes shifted to the movers. "They are like frightened animals, running when there is danger. Many times I have killed the *pindalickovi*, but there is no pleasure in it for it is like slapping a child." He touched Brazos' chest. "Someday we may fight, you and I, but there will be no hate between us. Neither will the victor spit on the other. This is Apache land and those who live here must become like Apache. You are like Apache, Sun-in-the-Hair. You want to pass through Apache country? Tuscos agrees. No Apache will harm you."

Brazos understood this was a moment that might

151

never come again, and he seized it. Grasping Tuscos' thumb, he pressed his own tightly against it and then drove the point of his knife into their flesh so that the blood mingled. Tuscos grunted and smiled and his face lost its savagery. The dark eyes were warm. "We will meet across the river," he said. "I will watch for you."

Whirling, he shouted one word to his band and they melted quickly into the rocks. Martin came up after they had gone and said, "Brother to a goddamned Apache!" He spat.

Modry joined them, his heavy shoulders rounded. "We're ready," he said. New lines were etched in his face and his eyes looked dully over the land as if he wondered whether this was worth dying for.

"I'll take the point," Martin said and trotted away. When he disappeared around a far bend, Brazos signaled for the train to move and whips cracked and creaking wheels and clanking iron shoes on rock formed a mounting din. Dust rose thick again and Brazos went ahead until he was a hundred yards in the lead on the uphill side. Occasionally he saw Martin, a vague shape moving rapidly. Brazos turned his head often to observe the slow-moving train. He was not like these people, he told himself. The past did not mean anything to him; only the present concerned him. Tomorrow held no fears. He guessed that these people liked to be certain of everything, but in this land that was impossible.

The sun was high and hot, and sweat soaked his buckskins. The wound in his shoulder was healed now and except for an occasional twinge of discomfort when the weather changed, he could forget that he had it.

Strung out in a ragged line, the wagons moved at a snail's pace, the column of dust rising in a tan wave. He turned his head often to check their progress and the afternoon went by, slowly as though time were marching in half-step.

Jubal Caine came early the next morning and Martha Olroyd fixed his breakfast as he sat at the table and talked. "Jeb is real put out about the shootin'. He feels it ought to be handled legal-like at Ryker's store. He don't think you was justified in what you done."

Martha stopped stirring the scrapple. "Justified?" There was anger in her eyes. "Jubal, if a girl can't protect herself, then who the blazes is going to do it for her?"

"Don't get het up now," Jubal cautioned. "I see no real trouble in gettin' shed of this thing. Besides, makin' it legal-like is better, you'll see."

She dished the food on plates and sat down across from him. She picked at her food, then passed a hand across her forehead. "Jubal, I'm scared. Plain scared."

"Emma go home?"

"She's over to Ryker's store," Martha said, then gripped his sleeve. "What did Asa and Ray mean, that Brazos ain't comin' back? I'm fit to lose my mind, worryin' about it."

"Now, now. Brazos'll be back," Jubal said. "He's my boy and I guess he'll cut his own in any crowd."

She raised her eyes and looked at him. "Why did you say that? He's somethin', ain't he? Somethin' that no one else here is."

Jubal thought for a moment, then nodded. "Yeah, he's somethin', all right, but dogged if I know what it is. I've been tryin' to put my finger on it for a right smart spell, but it just circles and don't light." He finished his meal and poured a cup of coffee.

"I think he knows where he's goin'," Martha said.

153

"He's always chasin' in the hills, if that's what you mean," Jubal said. "Out there he sees and hears a mess of things nobody else can less'n he's half-horse, half-mountain lion."

"But how can you be sure he's comin' back? How can you, Jubal?" She cupped her hands around the coffee cup and sat quietly for a while. "Asa and Ray's been up to somethin', I know it. Maybe Brazos is scalped and dead by now; we don't know."

"They're alive," Caine said and finished his coffee. "I tried it in the hills a few times, but I didn't like it. It's godawful lonesome out there. A man gets a feelin' and he gets to lookin' at the rocks and hearin' noises." He shook his head. "A diff'rent kind of lonely out there, Martha. Takes a special kind of man to stand it. Martin and Brazos can take it, but then, they ain't alike either. Brazos, he listens to the wind talkin' and hears somethin' I don't. All I hear is a moanin' that makes chills run up'n down my spine." He got up and turned to the door. "Thanks for the breakfast and don't worry about Jeb McClintock."

"I'm the worryin' kind," Martha said and watched him walk back across the flats. She went to the door and leaned against it, her hand blocking the sun from her face. For a long time she stared at the ring of high mountains, then turned back inside and closed the door.

CHAPTER FIFTEEN

THE ONE-TIME LEADER OF THE SETTLEMENT, JEB McClintock, felt that he had been cheated out of his just due, and he had been quietly casting about for some method by which he could restore himself to his former

154

position. The shooting of his son was such a windfall that he forgot to mourn Asa's death. He laid his plans carefully and when his anger was whipped to a sharp-edged fury, decided to act.

He realized that any course he chose must be designed to leave him in undisputed power in the settlement. He thought he saw such an opportunity through this fate-bestowed accident and the vulnerability of Martha Olroyd. Being Brazos' woman, Martha would be considered immune from reprisals.

But Jeb McClintock thought that he could dispel this belief and, by bringing Martha to justice, break Brazos' grip on these people. A simple people, they would respond more quickly to the strong hand of discipline than to a loose form of justice where every man took care of his own. In his own mind, McClintock felt sure that Ray Olroyd had talked Asa into going to Brazos' cabin. Damn Ray Olroyd anyway! The coward was now hiding out in the hills . . .

Entering his cabin, McClintock tossed his hat on the table and looked around for his sons. His wife sat by the fireplace mending one of his frayed shirts. "Where's Antrim and Roan?" he asked.

"Out in the barn. There's a mare that needs shoes."

She put the shirt aside and watched him with eyes red from crying. Women were like that—full of tears when there was nothing to be gained by crying. Asa was dead and that was all there was to it.

"Never mind the mare," he said. He went to the front door and thrust his head out. "Antrim! Roan!" He came back into the big room, his boots whacking the packed dirt floor. A moment later the two boys came in from the barn. He said, "That likker-swillin' Ray Olroyd's skedaddled. Can you find him?"

155

"I guess we could," Antrim said. "He may be across the river."

"Then go after him. Bring him back here to me, you understand?"

"What if he don't want to come?" Roan asked. "Martin'll be back any day now and he can add two and two, same's the rest of us."

"Dammit," McClintock said, "I don't aim to argue about it. Now you find him, or I'll skin the hides off both of you."

"Asa was mine too," his wife said in a dull voice. "McClintock, ain't we got enough trouble?"

"I know what I'm doin'," he said.

"I ain't blamin' the girl," she went on. "Ray was a he-cat when he had a jug. I believe Jubal when he told how it happened."

"And I'll prove they're lies if I have to hang the girl," he said. "Was I to bring order now, I'd be in charge again. I've got the President's commission."

"I want no more trouble," she repeated. "McClintock, I don't have a friend in the settlement, but Martha's treated me best. I'm tired of this. Let it go."

"Agh," he said and expressed his opinion of a woman's judgment. He motioned his sons away and they went to the lean-to barn and saddled horses. McClintock watched them from the doorway as they rode out and soon passed over the first rise. Then he took his rifle and went to the barn.

Forney was ten and big for his age. He had his father's angular face and some of his intolerance; he had listened well to his father's frequent bitter discourses. "Get your gun," McClintock said. "We have a job that needs to be done."

"All right," Forney said and went across the yard at a

156

trot. McClintock waited for the boy in the barn doorway and from there he could hear his wife's rising voice, questioning Forney. But the youngster just walked away and left his mother talking to herself. When he came back, McClintock had him saddle two horses and then they mounted. From the wall, the old man took a coil of rope and rode with it in his hand. For a mile he held to silence, but when they neared Brazos' cabin, he said, "We're goin' to make an arrest legal, son. However, if any harm should befall me, shoot to kill. Remember your brother Asa. Remember him well for he was a fine lad. Spirited, but fine."

"Sure, Pa."

They were a hundred yards from the cabin when the door opened and Martha came out. She stood with her hands on her hips, watching the McClintocks approach. Emma came out to see who was coming, but Martha pushed her back inside. McClintock stopped but did not dismount. He was ten feet from the doorway and his long cap-lock rifle was held casually across his bony chest. "I'm placin' you under arrest," he said and watched the surprise widen Martha's eyes.

"You don't have to do that," Martha said. "I'll be there when you have your stupid trial."

We'll go accordin' to the law," he said. "Better come along now with no fuss."

"I'll give you one hell of a fuss," Martha promised and began to inch back inside. McClintock spoke to his son.

"Stop her!"

The youngster swung his rifle to his shoulder and' the lock clicked loudly as he brought the hammer to full cock. Martha drew her breath in sharply and stood unmoving. Over the barrel, Forney's eyes were as cold and hard as his father's.

"He has his instructions," McClintock said and uncoiled the rope, fashioning a slip knot on one end. He shifted his horse with knee commands and dropped the noose over Martha's head. Instinctively she raised her hands and ducked her head to pull free, and McClintock backed his horse quickly and the rope tightened. The sudden jerk brought her to her knees and from that position she raised her head and looked at him.

"You're an evil, hatin' old man!"

"Justice is going to be served," he said coldly. "Get up and walk or I'll drag you to Ryker's." He turned his horse and Martha gained her feet in time to maintain slack in the rope. Forney dropped to one side and fell in behind her, the rifle cocked and ready.

They came across the flats slowly and from Jubal Caine's cabin, Brazos' mother came out, saw the procession, and went back inside after her husband. Jubal had his pistol on when he left the cabin. He cut across the flats toward Ryker's and was waiting when McClintock came up and dismounted.

The people were assembled in front of Ryker's building. Mrs. Olroyd looked at her daughter and there was tragedy etched in the older woman's face. Jethro and Clem, Martha's younger brothers, were standing near the wall, solemn-faced and unsure of themselves.

McClintock held up his hand when Sykes and Povy came from the store. "All of you—hear this for I'll not repeat it. I am binding this woman over for trial. Ryker, I'm placin' the prisoner in your room for safekeepin'."

"No!" Mrs. Olroyd said in a pleading voice. She took a step toward her daughter and Forney swung the rifle toward her.

"Stop," he said and everyone looked at him.

Jubal Caine spoke. "Seems that you're tryin' to prove somethin' here, Jeb. I see no reason for bringin' the girl in like this, with a rope around her."

"I'll decide how it's to be done," he said. "Your son swayed these people to him in a moment of excitement, but he is off again, into the hills instead of tending to his business. As the President's servant, I'm takin' over again."

"Figured it was somethin' like that," Caine said. "Better make that kid of yours put up that rifle before he kills someone."

"He can handle the rifle," McClintock said. He swept the group with his eyes, once more the leader. "Gather in the store this afternoon. We'll listen then to the evidence."

"This is too damned much for my stomach," Jubal Caine said. "McClintock, there'll be no trial until my boy gets back."

"Don't interfere with me!" McClintock warned. "I'll run the settlement the way I see fit."

Caine raised his attention to Forney, who still held his rifle on Mrs. Olroyd. Caine said, "Put that away, Forney."

"Don't order my son around," McClintock said, but Jubal Caine moved with surprising swiftness. He grabbed the muzzle and thrust it down. The gun went off, spraying dirt and noise, then Caine had it and was swinging it like an ax. The blow caught Forney across the stomach and swept him off the horse.

Jeb McClintock's mad roaring warned Caine in time to turn, but Sykes struck McClintock with a crutch, staggering him. McClintock's rifle went off when he released it and the ball plowed into Ryker's wall.

159

Forney was flat on his back, moaning and moving his legs slightly. The old man was standing away from Sykes, one arm dangling. He watched Sykes with a deep hatred.

Jubal Caine took the rope off Martha and threw it on the ground. "We'll lock her up," he said, "but by God there'll be no trial until Brazos gets back."

McClintock let out a long sigh and nodded, his anger too great to permit speech. He looked at Forney, who was trying to sit up, but he did not offer to help him. He walked over to where the boy lay and stood rifle-straight, tilting only his eyes downward. "Get up," he said, and when Forney started to cry, shouted, "Get up, I said!"

Leaning forward, Forney shook his head slowly from side to side. The boy's hands moved in the dust, leaving tracks like some alien animal. This was the last straw for Jeb McClintock and he turned away from his son in disgust. Jubal Caine watched this, shocked, and when McClintock mounted, Caine picked up the rope, balled it and threw it. It struck McClintock's back and dribbled off the horse's rump. The old man turned slowly and looked at Caine, then bent from the saddle and retrieved it. "Thank you," he said coldly. "It is the only good rope I have left and I'll need it to hang her with." He turned his horse and moved back across the flats at a walk.

Forney was still making pawing motions in the dust and Jubal lifted him, motioning with his head for the two Olroyd boys to come and take him. They took Forney into the building, Ryker and his two half-grown daughters moving quickly out of the way. When they were all inside, Mrs. Olroyd spoke to Jubal Caine. "Does she have to be locked up?"

"We made a bargain," Caine said. He touched Martha

160

on the arm and led her into Ryker's storeroom. The place was a bare cubicle with a few sacks of grain stacked in one corner. Some old boxes sat in the middle of the floor. "Don't worry, girl, everythin' will turn out all right."

"I'll be fine," Martha said and sat down on the grain sacks. Her composure shattered, and she braced her elbows on her knees and covered her face with her hands. She cried in a dry, choked way. For several minutes she sat like this, then she wiped her eyes with the back of her hand. "Don't worry about me."

"Brazos'll be comin' in tomorrow or the next day," Jubal said. "I know—but Asa was wrong, you'll see."

"You take Emma home with you," Martha said. "She'll be afraid out there alone."

"I'll do that," he said and shifted his feet. "A shame there's no window in here. I'll have Ryker put a chain across the door so's it'll be open a few inches." He went out and moved to the front of the store, drawing Ryker aside. Martha's brothers were outside with Forney. Mrs. Olroyd's face was drawn with worry. Finally Ryker went into the back room with a length of chain and spiked it across the door so that the panel opened six inches, but no more. He connected the ends of chain with a brass padlock.

With that finished, he went outside where the others waited.

CHAPTER SIXTEEN

THE FIGHT WITH THE COMANCHES WAS THREE DAYS behind them now and all but forgotten. There were other things to occupy them. The man who had been seriously

161

wounded died and had to be buried. The next day Tattersal's lead ox fell and broke a leg. Brazos shot him and had him dragged to the side of the trail. Late the same day, Wikersham's wife was injured when a wheel sheared while crossing a rock stretch and the wagon toppled on her. A full day was wasted here, a brutal day with her crushed legs beneath the heavy wheel. Into the night men worked and cursed, trying to free her. The sun died and a cool wind came through the canyon and the sounds of the moving train were replaced with new ones. There was the deep grunting of men, the woman's moan of intense pain that came from her throat in wild spasms, the clank of steel against rock and the splintering of poles used for peevys.

Once the wagon was raised enough, but the pole broke before they could remove her and the agony commenced anew. Finally the night ended and she was released. Brazos set her legs and transferred her to a wagon where a cradle had been suspended between top bows.

Trouble dogged them with maddening regularity. The next afternoon, Calhoun got drunk and fell out of a wagon, fracturing his left arm. And that night one of Modry's youngsters mistook a member of the train for an Indian and shot him through the buttocks.

Tempers grew shorter as each day passed and the train moved more slowly than it had the day before. At the end of the eighth day, Brazos began to grow concerned for they were still two days from Ryker's and not making much progress. His two-wheeled carts were weathering the rough trail without difficulty, but the wagons were in sad shape. Martin, became more and more withdrawn and finally camped alone, speaking to no one. Twice, Brazos went to him, but Martin was in a surly mood and, thereafter, Brazos left him completely alone.

With their numbers cut by conflict and accident, the movers were in poor shape when Brazos halted them on the crest of a rise and gave them their first look at Ryker's settlement. The women left the wagons and stood in a ragged line. Children romped through the thick grass while the men stared at the valley. To those who were injured, gentle hands lifted them and held them so they too could see.

The thirteen difficult days faded and men turned their thoughts ahead to the chores that must be done before winter. Brazos saw a crowd gathering by Ryker's and judged that Martin must have told of the movers' coming; he had left two days before and had not come back.

The afternoon sun was hot as they navigated the last slope. Dust became a following cloud as the heavy wheels and double-shoes of the oxen tore the grass. Looking back at the slash that marked their trail, Brazos decided that his road was now well marked. The next party would have it easier. Looking at the waving sea of grass, a man would think that it could not be penetrated, for a plow would hardly touch it. But wagon wheels ground it down and once cut, it did not grow again.

By the time the sun touched the high rim of the surrounding mountains, the train was on the flats not more than a mile from Ryker's. The entire settlement was waiting there, and when Brazos drew the wagons in a line, Jeb McClintock stepped forward.

He wore a dark suit, threadbare at the elbows and cuffs, but he had combed his hair and beard and wore the mantle of dignity well. He approached Modry and engaged the big man in talk while Brazos searched the crowd for Martha. The women from the settlement soon joined the women in the train and there was the happy murmur of new voices as they all talked at once. Jubal Caine came over to Brazos and touched him on the arm. "Things has happened since you left."

"Where's Martha?" Brazos swung his head from side to side. "What kind of happenin's?"

Jubal recounted the shooting of Asa McClintock in a matter-of-fact voice and Brazos listened, his eyes flinty. He waited until his father was through, then tried to step around him and go to Jeb McClintock.

Jubal held his arm. "Now take it easy," he said. "You gain nothin' that way."

"Then I'll do it the other way. Where is she?"

Jubal sighed, for he knew his son. "Locked in Ryker's storeroom."

Brazos pivoted on his heel and entered the store, going into the back with long, angry steps. He saw the chain and padlock. Martha stirred inside and said, "Brazos?" Her face appeared along the six-inch crack, then she sat down weakly and began to cry. "Asa—said you wasn't comin' back?"

Brazos stopped trying to pull the chain from the ringbolts. "What?"

She raised her head and tears made runnels through the dirt on her face. "Asa said that. What did he mean, Brazos?"

"I'm not sure," he said, reaching inside to touch her. "I'll be right back, Martha. I'll get you out of here."

"I'm not afraid now," she said, her voice following him as he went back through the store. He found Ryker by the door, and the man was all smiles.

"I've been looking at my supplies, boy. God, but you made a good trade there."

"To hell with the trade," Brazos snapped. "Where's my Colt's pistols?"

"Why," Ryker said, "Asa McClintock took 'em ten days ago. He promised to pay handsome for 'em."

"You damn fool, Ryker," Brazos said and went into the back room. Martha had her face pressed against the crack in the door. Her hair was loose and fallen around her shoulders. "You're gettin' out of here," he said and drew his Colt's pistol. "Get away from the door."

He cocked and sighted quickly. The pistol reared in his hand and the heavy lock jumped. Someone outside yelled and a shiny indentation marked the lock. A second shot broke it and it fell to the floor with a sharp clank. Brazos kicked the chain clear of the ringbolt and threw the door wide open.

Leading Martha to the front of the store, Brazos stopped as Jeb McClintock came in, the others crowding after him. McClintock said, "Caine, this time you have gone too far. You are under arrest, by the power invested in me by the President of the Texas Republic."

"Go plumb to hell," Brazos said. "I got some business with you that won't wait." He left Martha and faced McClintock. "Asa got what was comin' to him, and I only regret I didn't catch him first."

"Now see here. My boy intended no harm to the—"

"I ain't talkin' about that," Brazos interrupted. "You hear me out, Jeb, then hunt yourself a damn hole and hide in it." Brazos shot a question at Ryker without turning his head. "Where did my Colt's pistols go, the ones I offered to Jeb McClintock?"

"I told you Asa took 'em," Ryker said. "What the hell's goin' on around here?"

"We were ambushed by Comanches," Brazos said. "The people with Modry'll tell you about it. How do

165

you suppose them Comanches knew we was comin' through there? Because a white man told 'em!"

"That's a very grave charge," McClintock said slowly. "Very grave."

"I found percussion caps, Jeb. The Comanches had a surprise brush with the Apaches and our friend was there. Those percussion caps fitted a Colt's pistol."

McClintock's eyes widened as understanding came to him. He raised his fist to strike and Ryker grabbed his arm. "Better hear this out!"

"I'll not stand here and have my son's name spit upon!" McClintock struggled against Ryker's grip and Sykes grabbed the other arm, effectively holding him.

"Keep talkin'," Ryker said softly. "We want to hear this."

"Pa says neither Ray or Asa's been around the settlement since we've been gone, 'cept for that one night. Now Ray's pistol is a .28 bore. Martin and Pa's got .36 calibers, but I know where Martin was and you know where Pa was. So that leaves Asa McClintock, who had my old set of pistols." Brazos speared Jeb McClintock with his eyes. "You got your guts lockin' Martha up and makin' a big stink when your own son's been sellin' the settlement out to Esqueda and th' Comanches. What you got to say now? You're so damned full of talk."

McClintock was a sick man. The color drained from his cheeks and his hands trembled. He looked at the people crowding the store, at the ones he knew and at the new ones who were judging him in this moment. Finally he spread his hands in a helpless gesture of defeat and turned, elbowing his way through the crowd.

Brazos said, "Before I went to Fort Davis you voted me to lead this settlement and I didn't want the job then.

Now I've changed my mind and I'll take it. I got goods out there on my wagons. Goods you all need and I'll have it in my store for tradin'. We're goin' to have a road through the Apache country to Fort Davis and things is goin' to be better. But first, there's the matter of Esqueda. I never held with killin' the man because he was a Mex, but things can't go on; the raidin', the fightin' all the time. I've made friends with the Apaches and I'm goin' after Esqueda. I'm goin' to root him out of his nest."

They went outside to digest this. Jubal Caine lingered until he saw that Martha and Brazos wanted to do some talking. He closed the door behind him.

Martha tried to smooth the wrinkles from her dress and straighten her hair but the attempt was unsuccessful. She said, "I ought to be all prettied up for you, but look at me. Locked in a feed room."

"You're pretty as a spotted pup," he said. "What was Asa tryin' to do?"

"What do you think?"

"Guess I know," he said. "Was Ray there too?"

She nodded. "You think he was with Asa when he tried to ambush you and got Apaches instead?"

"Not then," he said softly, "but he was with the Comanches before that. I'm sure sorry, Martha, but I got to find Ray."

"To kill him for what he's done?"

"I'd bring him back alive if I could," Brazos said. "I ain't like Martin."

"No, you're not."

He touched her gently and she pressed against him. For a moment they remained like this, then Brazos stepped away from her. "Now you keep your mouth shut," he said. "Martin's home now but he'll figure to

167

go after Ray too; he's got a reason now. I got to get to Ray before he does or there'll just be another dead man." He pulled her to him for his kiss, then released her. "You go on home now and wait for me. Put the goods on the shelf and there's some new dresses for you."

"Home?" She smiled. "I've been dreaming of the day when you'd get back and it would really be home. But it seems that there's always something coming between us."

"You think I like this waitin'?"

"No," she said. "You're an impatient man, Brazos, and I've wondered if you'll be a rough one."

"You'll soon find that out," he said and kissed her again. The crowd was still congregated in front of Ryker's when Brazos struck out toward the hills and Martin's place. When he topped the first rise and dropped over the other side he changed direction, angling toward the Rio Grande ten miles beyond. Cutting across the lower spur of another valley, he paused on the sidehill to look back. He was leaving a faint trail in the grass but that couldn't be helped. A full darkness was not more than fifteen minutes away and he pressed on, haste like a hand at his back.

Darkness was falling when Martin and Emma crossed his yard and went into the cabin. There were chores to be done, wood to cut and a meal to fix. It was nearly eight o'clock when they finished eating.

The candle in the center of the table sputtered. A feeble yellow light tried to brighten the room. Martin took off his buckskin shirt and washed himself in a half-filled tub. The wound in his side was healed to a pink scar and he touched it while drying himself.

Emma sat at the table, watching him lather his face

for his shave. During the trip from Fort Davis he had postponed such niceties but now he whetted his Barlowe knife and slowly removed his beard. When he finished his skin glistened and he turned to face her. "I heard the talk. Where's Ray Olroyd?"

She was mute for a moment, her fingers moving idly in her lap. "I don't know, Martin." She tried a wan smile. "You haven't kissed me. Don't you like to kiss me any more?"

He pushed this aside, saying, "Emma, I want th' truth. Where is he? In the hills?"

"I told you I didn't know."

"I'll kill him sure as hell," Martin said. His face grew hard and his eyes were like agates. "No man fools with my woman!"

"Martin, do you love me?"

His head came around sharply. "Why do you ask that?"

"Would you kill him because you loved me, or because you couldn't stand anyone takin' what was yours?"

He stepped toward her and jerked her to him. "That woman of Brazos' has been puttin' ideas into your fool head." He kissed her, a crushing pressure of his lips. His hands explored her, pulled her dress from her shoulder.

She slid her lips away and said, "Martin, don't take from me—let me give."

His hunger was demanding and he slipped an arm behind her knees and carried her to his bunk. The lamplight touched her eyes as he watched her and in their depths was the fire, the desire he had always hoped to read in a woman's eyes.

He kissed her again but this time he caused her no pain and her arms brushed the back of his neck, the pressure light and caressing. The flame from the candle

169

flickered and the light danced along the rough wall.

She was asleep when he packed his parfleche and softly went outside. There was a faint moon, good for traveling, and he struck out across the land, working his way up the slopes toward the Rio Grande. For over an hour he made his way southeast until he breasted a high ridge, there pausing to rest. He had been making good time but the hour was late. After a moment, he shifted his parfleche to his shoulder and struck out again.

By the time the sun began to rinse the sky of darkness, Brazos Caine had picked up the trail of the McClintock boys' horses. In a land where horses went unshod, McClintock stubbornly clung to the habit of shoeing although the need was a thousand miles and more to the east in the cobblestones of Richmond or the baked-clay back roads flanking the Tennessee.

The land here was wild and thickly brushed. Stunted trees clung to the down-sloping hills and ahead a mile or two lay the Rio Grande. From the tracks, Roan and Antrim were making broad sweeps along the ridges and Brazos was puzzled by this shuffling. He spent most of the morning following them until the pattern of their movement became clear to him. Then he made a camp high in the rocks and settled down to wait.

From strips of buckskin off his shirt he made small snares and caught a rabbit, which he skinned and stripped to dry in the sun. Resetting the snare, he caught two more before mid-afternoon. Building a minute fire of twigs, he cooked the meat and tucked it inside his shirt. Twice during the afternoon he saw movement, but they were Indians, not the McClintock boys. Never did he get a clear view, but what he saw convinced him they were Apaches, not Comanches.

According to his calculations, the McClintock boys

should show themselves sooner or later as they switched back. Patience was important in tracking; heedless movement could cost a man his life.

By late afternoon, when his wait proved fruitless, he left his place and moved into the rolling slopes below. The deepening dusk made traveling slow and he studied the land for any sign that would lead him to Ray Olroyd. He felt sure that the McClintocks were after Ray, but he could not figure out why. Full night caught him overlooking the last downsweep that flanked the Rio Grande.

The Apaches he had seen earlier in the day fell into this mental picture he was forming, for along the bank he discovered the tracks where the McClintocks had crossed. He also found the bare spot that the Apaches had wiped clean and this told him that they were on the McClintock boys' trail. From this vague sign he read the complete story of the hunter and the hunted. He hurried along the brush-lined bank until he came to a rock outcropping and then let himself down into the water. His pistols, powder and caps were hoisted over his head to keep them dry.

With the sun gone, a deep chill descended and he emerged on the Mexican side, shivering. He was certain now that Ray Olroyd was also across the river. He tried to untangle the movements of those men in his mind. There seemed to be no doubt in Ray Olroyd's mind, judging from his track, just where he was going, and for a time, Brazos wondered if the McClintocks didn't know too, for they followed Olroyd unerringly to the river. Then they became confused, wandering back and forth, trying to pick up the trail. These things he had read carefully and now tried to sort out.

His old suspicions of Asa and Ray returned. They

never worked, and were rarely around the settlement. There was only one place for a man to go and that was into the hills, but neither was a trapper. He thought of the pistols, and other things, like a full jug of whiskey all the time and the money to buy more, the suspicions slowly crystalizing. Asa and Ray had been playing Clay's selling game. This wasn't hard to see when a man put his mind on it. The Comanches would raid when the settlement was unprotected, and for this information, these two were left alone when they crossed the river. But what did they do about the Apaches? Brazos decided to ask Tuscos when he saw him.

The two younger McClintock boys, Brazos decided, were not in this, and he was glad of it. They were after Olroyd for another reason and the thought of their catching up with him was unpleasant. They were young and dumb and would expect to find a friend. Olroyd would kill them and leave them lay. He supposed that Ray and Asa were working with Esqueda too; the gold would come from the Mexican.

He moved away from the river and worked his way southeast again, traveling nearly four miles before taking a high position in the rocks. The night was faintly light and he pillowed his head in his arms and slept.

He could not say what brought him awake and alert, but he sensed danger. There was no single sound in the night that had warned him that he was not alone. Crickets interrupted their song and the tenor of the wind seemed to change. He drew his long-barreled pistol and cocked it beneath his armpit to muffle the click of hammer-notch. Breathing through his open mouth to make no sound, he waited for what seemed an indefinite time, then a shadow shifted to his right and he swung

172

the gun muzzle around. Some men would have shot, but he held his fire while the man moved closer. A break in the clouds allowed a pale shaft of moonlight to shoot earthward and it glinted grayly on the rocks. The clouds closed again, but the brief light had been sufficient.

Brazos said, "Jesus, Martin—what the hell you doin' ?"

There was a grunt of surprise, then Martin slipped into place beside Brazos Caine. Carefully uncocking his gun, Brazos replaced it in the hip scabbard.

"I been havin' one hell of a time trailin' you," Martin said. He smelled strongly of sweat, and weariness rounded his shoulders. He jerked his head toward the river. "Olroyd cross over?"

"The McClintock boys too," Brazos said softly and told Martin about the Apaches.

The man grunted and got to his feet. "I didn't come here to rescue no damn McClintock. Olroyd's the one I want."

"Because he messed with your woman or because he's workin' for Esqueda?"

"Tell me about that," Martin invited and hunkered down again. He grunted occasionally as Brazos talked. When he was through, Martin said, "That son of a bitch."

Brazos studied this man in the darkness. "He ain't the only white man that's sold us out, Martin. There was others before him."

Martin stiffened and he stared at Brazos with eyes that were steel drills. Finally he relaxed. "I'm interested in gettin' Ray Olroyd."

The talk was finished and Brazos led the way from the rocks. For better than an hour they moved across the valley floor, following a crooked stream that cut racing slots in bare rock. At last they came to a sandy stretch of beach and Brazos studied the current carefully. He understood that they would have to enter upstream and let the current carry them to the curve on the far bank. But a horse would swim straight across, not drift, and if any sign of the McClintock boys was to be picked up, it would be upstream. After removing his weapons, Brazos entered and felt the current pull him. He half-paddled, half-drifted and finally felt his knees scrape bottom. He and Martin emerged dripping on the other side.

Brazos searched and found sign in nothing more than a blade of grass crushed until the juice was fresh and slick on the shoot. He could not see because of the darkness; he tasted the shoot. He knew that the Apaches were ahead of him, for there actually was no trail to follow. They had wiped it out cleverly. But nature has rhyme and reason to her structure and when man erases a trail he disrupts this rhyme, thereby pointing out the flaws he wishes to conceal. Brazos found horse droppings but this did little to cheer him. The Apaches could run down a horse if need be and apparently they were having no difficulty keeping up with the McClintocks.

They ran ahead now. Brazos did not search for bits of sign, often passing over a mark in the ground that a less experienced tracker would have stopped to ponder over. With the quarry moving fast, he had no time to worry over each clue. The establishment of direction was the important thing, for a man traveled over virgin land with well-defined landmarks in mind. Once Brazos had established this direction in his mind, he moved more swiftly. Angling to the right, he raised a lonely peak in the distance and made it the target for his march. Midnight found both men deep in this hostile land and Brazos paused when he found a trampled spot, indicating that horses had stood here for some time.

"Three hours ago," Brazos said, feeling the ground. He moved off again, his long stride eating miles.

The first touch of dawn found them on the edge of the flats and before them stretched the broken slopes of a small mountain. For hours he had seen no sign of the Apaches and this formed a worry in his mind. With the approaching day not far off and the grayness thinning by the minute, Brazos drove himself harder, traversing quickly a steep slope. His muscles were aching and his eyes burned. A glance back showed a well-worn Martin straining to keep up.

Brazos did not search for Apache sign for he knew their ways and moved toward the high ground. High above water, with a clear view for miles around; that was where he would find them. The light was thin now and there would soon be no more half-darkness to mask them. Even now they were in great danger of detection. Passing through an archway of rocks, Brazos kept to the bed of a dry wash that led toward the rim. At another time he would have used a circular route, but he lacked both leisure and energy. Reasoning it out, he decided that if the Apaches had the McClintocks—and they probably did—they would be amusing themselves and not keep too sharp a lookout.

Dawn turned into a pink stain that spread to a brighter and brighter shade. They were near the top now and Brazos halted, pointing down. They flattened themselves against the edge of a depression. In a cup-shaped ledge two Apaches hunkered down no more than twenty yards away. In the far distance, a cluster of adobe buildings crouched along the bank of a stream. Around them, the flatness of a larger valley stretched in all directions.

It was, Brazos realized, the stronghold of Emiliano

Esqueda. And the Apaches had camped practically at his doorstep.

CHAPTER SEVENTEEN

EMILLANO ESQUEDA HAD CHOSEN WELL THE SITE FOR his hacienda. There was a slight depression in the plain where the creek made a sharp bend and he had used it to hide the buildings. Anyone traveling across the vast floor would not see even the rooftops and since he would have no reason to climb the rocky promontory, the stronghold would remain as invisible as if it never existed. Further back along the trail, when the traveler was in high ground, this very range of peaks hid the plain from view.

"Pretty damned smart," Brazos murmured and turned his attention to the Apaches in the pocket below. He could see clearly now. They had prisoners; Roan and Antrim McClintock. The two boys were tied together, back to back, dirty strips of red cloth over their mouths. The Apaches were wearing warpaint, broad streaks of white and red across their cheeks. The sun appeared, slanting bright light across the plain below.

Brazos studied the Apaches, then stood up.

The two guards on the rim saw him and whirled, their weapons raised, but Tuscos spoke one sharp word and Brazos came in, Martin trailing him. Brazos walked to the center of this depression but Martin sat down near the base of the rim, indicating by this that he wished to have nothing to do with the Apaches. Tuscos greeted Brazos and said, "Sun-in-the-Hair is welcome. Here are two from the *Pindalickoyi* settlement that hate all Indians. Much pleasure will be yours in seeing them die slowly."

"These boys are our friends and mean you no harm," Brazos said. "Does Tuscos make war on children?"

"If they are your friends, no harm will come to them," Tuscos said. "But we have followed them long and it was necessary to take them this way. There is another, an evil one, who has gone on ahead." He pointed to the adobe buildings tawny in the sunlight. "To the fortress of Esqueda. I could not let these babes go there. It would warn Esqueda that others are following."

"You got a good point there," Brazos said and hunkered down, his glance sweeping the Apache camp. There was nothing here but men and weapons. The Apaches liked to move fast and leave no trace behind. Their women and children were somewhere else, in a more permanent camp that a white man would never see. Brazos asked, "You know this white man, this evil one?"

"Well," Tuscos said. "He has given whiskey to my men in place of the *tiswin*. Bad whiskey. They drink, fight, die. Many Apache kill each other because of this man." He touched Brazos. "Sun-in-the-Hair, he is mine. I ask nothing more."

Brazos shot Martin a glance and the mountain man said, "Think quick and straight now."

"He'll roast Olroyd over a fire!"

"Ain't he got it comin'?" Martin asked dryly.

Brazos pondered this. Esqueda had used Olroyd and the man had been stupid enough to fall for it. Now Tuscos was asking for his life and Ray would die, slowly and agonizingly. Brazos supposed he could refuse, but this would create a rift between him and Tuscos. The safety and welfare of the settlement was at stake here. With Tuscos friendly, he would be in and out

177

of the settlement, trading, making friends with the settlers.

He said, "I give you the hand of a brother, Tuscos. He is yours to deal with."

The Apache leader spoke and the McClintock boys were released, the gags removed. They sat still for a few minutes, then stood up unsteadily. Antrim, the oldest, said, "Jesus, Brazos, but I been scared as hell!"

"Don't blame you none," Brazos told him. "Tuscos could have carved you up into bite-sized chunks." He stretched out on a flat rock and folded his hands behind his head.

Antrim McClintock pawed his foot around. "Heard what you said, or at least I got the drift. Ray's a white man. Ain't you goin' to rescue him from Esqueda?"

"He don't need it. He's been workin' with the Mexican."

"Jesus!" Antrim said. "You sure?"

"We're all sure," Brazos said. "There was someone else in this, Antrim. Your brother, Asa."

Anger smeared the boy's eyes. "That's a goddamn lie !"

Tuscos turned his head and looked sharply at the boy. Even Martin took his arm from across his face and stared. Brazos watched Antrim closely. The boy was ready to fight and if he had had a weapon handy, would have used it. "It's no lie," Brazos said softly. "Wish it was, Antrim, but Asa and Ray's sold us out."

"Why? What'd they get out of it?"

Brazos shrugged. "A little gold, maybe. Safety in case the settlement fell, and I think it was due to go under. We couldn't hold out much longer, Antrim, and I think both Asa and Ray wanted to be alive afterward. Some men put a heap of store in just livin'."

"This'll kill Pa," Antrim said softly, tears in his eyes.

"Better get some sleep," Brazos advised softly. "We'll be goin' on when it gets dark. Come if you want, or go back."

"This McClintock don't run from a fight," Antrim said, turning back to his younger brother.

Tuscos came over to Brazos and squatted. "I have nine men. We sleep now, but tonight we strike." The Apache's stolid face relaxed and he smiled. This was not, Brazos decided, the smile of a man who killed for love of killing, but the pleasure a man knows when his honor is about to be restored, his wrongs to be righted.

After Tuscos returned to his followers, Martin said, "That Tuscos is a smart bastard. He needs our guns. If he had rifles of his own, we'd be on our bellies and they'd be strippin' the skin off our backs inch by inch."

"Feelin' that way, you better not get behind Tuscos," Brazos said. "Th' temptation might be more'n you can resist."

"What you tryin' to say?"

"Don't kill him like you killed the Indian at Fort Davis; invite him to a pull at the jug, then shoot him in the back."

"Why, you son of a—" Martin rolled half-erect, then stopped. Brazos dropped his hand to his hip, whipping out his pistol.

"Whoa now," he said. "Guess you better not get behind me neither." Martin, held motionless by the gun, glared at Brazos. He kept his hands flat on the ground, his muscles tensed as if he were about to spring. "Now just come ahead if you feel like it," Brazos advised. "You might as well make your try now, 'cause you will sooner or later."

"I got no reason to harm you," Martin said. His breath whistled in his nose and he watched the gun Brazos held. "But you keep raggin' me, boy. A man can't take that." He smiled but it was only skin deep; his eyes remained dark and flat in expression. "I used to cotton to you like I did Clay, but lately . . . I sure don't understand it."

"You been a puzzle to me," Brazos said, "but a piece or two's dropped into place and I don't trust you any more."

"I've done nothing to you to make you feel that way. Seems like lately you been pushin' at me, tryin' to get me to fight. We had our fun together. No need to keep after me all th' damn time."

"Sure," Brazos said. "We been over the hills an' sniffed the wind, but we ain't the same. You're like a pet bear; I just can't trust you no more." He lowered the gun to his leg and held it there. "I've been thinkin' about Clay. About what a no-good son of a bitch he must have been to sell out McClintock and Esqueda both."

Martin looked like a man belly-kicked. His eyes grew vacant and glassy and it was several minutes before he spoke. "I've killed a mess of men because they knew that, kid. So I'm givin' you warnin' now; don't ever stop watchin' your back."

"I never intended to," Brazos said and moved to another spot where he could lie facing Martin and still have a rock wall at his back.

Night was only moments away when Brazos woke and found Tuscos squatted by his side. Dark hair hung to the Apache's shoulders and a filthy sweat band kept it out of his eyes. "The hour of travel is here," Tuscos said softly. The sun was well down behind the hills and the red sky turned to a soft pink and then a deepening gray-blue.

Brazos ate some of the jerky that he carried inside his shirt and quenched his thirst from a skin waterbag. Martin stirred and Tuscos drew a rough map in the dirt. "Many times I have seen the fortress of Esqueda. The walls are thick and high but on a man's shoulders it would be possible to climb. One gate, and it can be opened only from inside." He drew a square on each of the four corners. "Wagon guns; they point out."

"Where's the powder shed?" Brazos asked.

"I know not," Tuscos said. "Back of the hacienda is the barracks and stable, like the soldiers at Fort Davis. To get in will not be easy, Sun-in-the-Hair."

"We'll get in," Brazos said and rubbed the back of his hand across his face. He stood up and this was the silent signal to leave. To Martin, he said, "I ain't worried much about you shootin' me now, because you need me to get Esqueda. But just keep away from *me*; I don't need *you*."

He turned and went to the head of the column with Tuscos. The two McClintock boys stayed somewhere in the center, surrounded by Apaches. Martin brought up the rear alone.

They moved in a string across the flats and night shrouded them. Brazos turned his head often and looked back for he did not trust Martin now in spite of what he had said. He could see the vague shape of the McClintock boys, struggling to keep up and he was amused at the contrast between white and Apache. The Apache wasted no motion. He did not drive his legs up and down like the McClintocks. He walked with a waddle, rolling his weight forward with each step, picking up his moccasins lightly.

There was no pause in the march and at the end of two hours, they were close to Esqueda's adobe fortress.

There was no moon and the darkness contained both danger and friendly protection. Squatting against the earth, they blended with the land.

Along the upper wall and on each corner, the black iron snouts of the three-pounders protruded. Brazos touched Tuscos and said, "If you can open the gate, I have a plan."

"The gate can be opened," Tuscos said.

On top of the wall, guards moved back and forth, muskets on their shoulders. Brazos watched them pace from corner to corner, then drew Tuscos close and talked softly. The Apache nodded and began to shift his men around. Brazos motioned for Roan and Antrim McClintock and they came up on their bellies. He talked some more and when the Apaches were deployed, moved closer to the high wall.

Two Apaches flitted like shadows and made the wall without detection. They were away from the gate and flattened against the sloped surface of the wall. Tuscos, with the remainder of his men, worked their way toward the gate, making no sound at all. Brazos left his place and, with the McClintock boys, joined the two Apaches along the wall. Tuscos watched this for when Brazos waved his hand, Tuscos made the startling sound of a wild bull snorting. On top of the wall, the guard's boots stopped and he listened. The sound came again, louder this time, then the guard walked away from the corner. As he did, one of the Apaches went up on the shoulders of the other and pulled himself up.

There was a murmuring run of talk as the two guards came together. Brazos hoisted himself up on the Apache's shoulders and found that his fingertips barely curled over the lip of the wall. A pair of hands grabbed his wrists and pulled him up.

Tuscos snorted again and one of the guards lifted his musket. A bowstring twanged and the arrow made a sodden thump as it found the guard's breastbone. The other man cried out and an arrow cut him short. He fell to the ground outside the gate.

Boots scraped on the wall as the McClintocks came up and over, then the Apache already on the wall dropped down and opened the main gate. From the other end of the rampart, men approached at a run and Brazos motioned for the McClintocks to help him as he ran the cannon back, the small wheels squeaking and rumbling on the metal rails. They succeeded in swinging it completely around and pointed it at the bobbing shapes racing toward them. There was no time to light a gunner's match; Brazos fired his pistol close to the touch hole and the cannon leaped, a sheet of flame arching from the muzzle. Screams tore the night silence and the McClintocks poured powder and ball down the barrel, ramming it home. Brazos sighted the gun around until it lay on the long adobe barracks. Tuscos was coming through the gate now and Roan McClintock lit the gunner's match.

The cannon leaped and roared again. Antrim was ready with a dripping swab while Roan pressed home another charge. A huge hole appeared in the barracks and splinters and broken timbers flew into the air. Brazos could hear the frantic yelling as Roan stepped back, the cannon loaded again. Another shot brought down one end of the building, trapping men who tried to escape to the yard. From the other side of the wall, a guard fired his musket, the ball singing off the cast-iron barrel of the cannon. "Keep this thing going," Brazos said, "but don't shoot into the hacienda. That's where we'll be."

He jumped down of the inside ramp and ran across the grounds. Behind him, the cannon boomed again, but from a different corner. He smiled; the McClintocks had swiveled another around.

The grounds were a hundred yards square and Esqueda's house lay in the exact center. Candlelight streamed from the windows and men ran out the arched doors, shouting, confused. Tuscos and his band were like scudding deer, skirting the main building. Along the wall the rattle of musket fire was weak, then a man cried out and fell heavily.

A moment later the McClintocks had swiveled another cannon and were pelting the end of the bunkhouse with chain-shot. Tuscos and his Apaches used the confusion and darkness to break through the other end. Knives flashed and men fell moaning.

Brazos approached the shrubs growing in profusion around the wide veranda, suddenly aware that Martin was by his right elbow. He held a pistol in one hand and a knife in the other.

The McClintock boys were pounding away with their cannon and the sounds of battle rolled like thunder. Tuscos ran around the back side of the house and came onto the porch. Sweat, mingling with the paint, made bright streaks down his face.

Brazos was nearest the open arch that led into the house and he pulled his other gun, stepping into the streaming candlelight. The main hallway was empty and he looked quickly into the first room. A fleeting movement from the other end caught his eye and he dove to one side as a pistol cracked. The bullet pocked the wall and then Ray Olroyd ran across the hall as Brazos snapped an answering shot. Olroyd vanished into a room and when Brazos started forward, Tuscos flung up his arm. "Your promise!" He ran forward, his fisted knife catching the light from the wall brackets. Outside, the crackle of musket fire blended with the boom of cannon, then a deep explosion shook the building and plaster sifted down from the ceiling.

"Powder magazine," Brazos said. "The McClintocks must have found it with a shot."

The house seemed vacant now, but somewhere in back, a pistol cracked and then a man yelled once. "Olroyd's done," Martin said and stepped deeper into the hallway. Heavy drapes hung from the ceiling and plants grew in large urns along the base of the floor. There was an arch opening up on the left and Brazos moved toward it, his pistols cocked and ready. The fight outside seemed far away, the sounds of it almost swallowed by the drapes. Through the arch they had entered, a bright light made leaping shadows in the yard as the powder magazine set buildings on fire.

This huge room had a fireplace at one end. Brazos looked around carefully and then walked to the center of it and stood. A moment passed before he realized that a man sat in the deep chair before the fireplace. Brazos moved quickly to one side, motioning for Martin to skirt the other side. The man in the chair stirred and said, "I cannot move, señores."

Brazos put a long table between himself and the chair, approaching with pistol poised. He stopped, shocked, and stared at the man. The man was Esqueda, who had terrorized the border country, but he was now a pitiful sight. The bullet Brazos had once fired had been lodged where no probe could reach and Esqueda's face was wan and drained of color. When he moved his eyes, it was with great effort and Brazos stifled an impulse to step forward and inform him that he was dying.

Esqueda's angular face was small-boned and the skin was filled with blue veins. He looked at Martin, who stood on his right. "I have long expected you," he said softly. He sat quietly and the sounds of the fighting came into the building. The pop of musketry had diminished to almost nothing.

From another part of the house, boots thumped on the tile floor and Antrim McClintock called out, "Brazos? Where the hell you at, Brazos?"

"In here," Brazos said and the McClintock boys came in.

"Jesus," Roan said, "the Apaches are pullin' out!"

"Tuscos got Olroyd," Antrim said. "They was all troopin' for the gate, what was left of 'em." He saw Esqueda in the chair and came around for his look. "Hell, he ain't much, is he?"

"There's enough life in him to jump when my bullet hits him," Martin said. He had his pistol in his hand, but not pointed at Esqueda.

The Mexican moved his eyes to Brazos. "Would you waste a bullet on a dying man?" His hands picked at the fringe of his lap robe, thin hands like the claws of a bird.

"Kill him and let's get out of here." Antrim said.

"There's death in his eyes now," Brazos said. "Let him sit here and look at the ruins."

"I want to watch him die," Martin said. "It will give me pleasure."

A smile flitted across Esqueda's lips and lifted the ends of his mustache. "There will be no pleasure for you, for I am not like your brother. He was a disappointment to me, Martin, for he screamed like a woman."

Martin's jaws clenched until the muscles bunched beneath the skin. His gun came around and his thumb

186

curled over the hammer.

Brazos yelled, "Don't, Martin! So help me, I'll kill you if you shoot him!"

These two men locked eyes and stood unmoving. Esqueda's hands shifted in his lap and his voice was gentle. "You find that you cannot spit on Emiliano Esqueda, eh?" He inclined his head toward Martin. "But he can spit. He would spit on God because He also knows of his brother's black heart."

Martin snarled something and then the robe in Esqueda's lap jumped and a smoldering hole appeared in it. Smoke came out in a rank, gray cloud. Martin was flung back and half fell into a table. His pistol went off into the floor, then he slipped down and Esqueda dropped his single-shot coach pistol. Roan lifted his rifle quickly, but Brazos shouted, "No!"

Esqueda was tipping forward in his chair and he fell slowly and rolled onto his back. His eyes were wide and vacant, focused on the ceiling beams as though he found them utterly fascinating. Martin lay back against the upended table, his stomach covered with blood. A trace of it appeared on his lips. He tried to lift himself but could not and fell back, his head rapping the floor. When Brazos bent over him, he asked, "Did you—kill him?"

"No," Brazos said and listened to Martin's labored breathing. "He got you good, Martin. You won't make it."

Sweat lay in beads on Martin's forehead. His heels drummed the floor and his arms twitched. "Don't leave—him alive. Don't leave—anyone alive to know —about Clay."

"*I* know what he was," Brazos said softly. "Captain Travers at Fort Davis knows. You'd never have been

187

able to kill 'em all, Martin, 'cause somebody always knows." Brazos slipped his leg under Martin's head for a pillow. "You spent your life on your brother Clay, Martin, an' you wasted it. Esqueda did you a favor by killin' him." He tried to lift Martin, but a dullness was creeping into the man's eyes and he stared vacantly at Brazos. Here was the tragedy, Brazos decided. The burning shame Martin must have lived with and tried so wrongly to hide. And now he would die never knowing how wasted his effort had been. Clay, who thought of no one, who had lied, cheated, betrayed without conscience, now robbed Martin of life. Esqueda, who had been a victim, was blameless, and Brazos supposed Martin could not help being what he was.

Martin's hand clawed at Brazos' shirt, fastening into the arm fringe. "Boy—I didn't know—how to set it right—what Clay'd done." He coughed, a spray of blood darkening Brazos' shirt front. "We had—fun. Listenin' to—th' wind."

He sagged then and Brazos let him lie flat. The two McClintock boys were standing by the long table, their faces grave. Roan said, "What th' hell's that about?"

"A man just died for nothin'," Brazos said. "Th' last of a long line of men."

"Huh," Roan said. "That son of a bitch is better off dead."

Brazos came erect quickly, on the verge of hitting Roan. Instead he said, "You shut up. You don't know nothin', you understand? Nothin'!"

"Jesus, I only said—"

"Who wants to hear what you got to say!" Brazos shouted.

Through the windows the flickering firelight winked and Brazos turned and went out, Antrim and Roan at his heels. Dotting the yard, the bodies of Esqueda's Mexican followers lay in grotesque heaps. The stable was in flames, as was the shot-marked bunkhouse. Nearly half of the front wall was rubble and Brazos ran toward this.

Outside he struck out across the flats and set a killing pace until he realized that the McClintock boys could not keep up. He waited for them, turning again to hold his pace to a walk. A bright glow behind him told him that the fire had spread to the hacienda. The burning fortress was a signal that would summon every Comanche within thirty miles. But they had a head start and a few hours would find them at Tuscos' camp.

As the land began to slant upward, Brazos halted and said, "Wait here." He turned and began the steep climb. Tuscos had chosen another spot to camp, as Brazos knew he would, but he had little difficulty finding it. When the faint odor of wood smoke came to him, he searched for the pocket and five minutes later entered the ring of firelight.

Tuscos had lost men; only four Apaches remained. On the ground, Ray Olroyd lay naked; he was staked, arms and legs outspread. Someone had already been at work with a knife and he lay gagging and wild-eyed with pain.

"Is the dark one below?" Tuscos asked. He meant Martin.

"He's dead," Brazos said. He made a point not to look at Olroyd lest he waver in his decision to keep out of this.

Tuscos said, "He has the heart of a chicken, but you are sorry you promised, is this not so?"

"I won't go back on it," Brazos said, looking around

189

for the horses he knew Tuscos had stolen. "I need three ponies," he said. "The Comanches are out now."

Tuscos spoke to one of his men and three horses were brought forward. He said, "With the dark one dead, there will be peace. Esqueda feared him."

"Esqueda killed him," Brazos said.

Tuscos nodded as though this was what he had expected. "The dark one was in league with death."

Mounting, Brazos took the lead rope of the other two horses and turned to leave. He forced himself to look at Ray Olroyd, to view the man's agony. A light glittered in Tuscos' eyes as he saw this quickly hidden compassion and he said, "To see someone suffer is to feel pain oneself; only the good can so feel it." He raised his hand and brushed the palm against the bone handle of Brazos' pistol. "Had I one of these, I would be a great chief."

Brazos pondered this, knowing that he could turn the request aside by riding out. But in Tuscos' voice there had been more than the longing for a superior weapon. He withdrew the Texas Colt and handed it to the Apache, butt first.

For a full minute, Tuscos turned the pistol over in his hands, then cocked it and pressed the muzzle against Olroyd's temple. The explosion was not loud and Olroyd jerked once and lay still. Handing the Colt back to Brazos, the Apache said, "To be merciful is to be great. The weapon has made me great."

"We'll meet again," Brazos said and turned the horse. He cut down-slope to where the McClintocks waited. They were asleep and he stirred them awake and they mounted. Then he retraced his former trail to the river crossing.

Through the night they alternately trotted and walked

the horses and dawn found them a few miles from the Rio Grande. In the broad daylight they swam the river again and emerged in the Republic of Texas. The McClintock boys expressed a desire to rest, but Brazos ignored them and pushed on. At noon Roan wanted to stop and cook a meal, but Brazos shook his head and traversed the last hill that led down into Ryker's settlement. He rode slack-bodied, his shoulders humped, and lines of weariness wrinkling the skin near his eyes and lips.

With Ryker's buildings in view, Brazos stopped his horse and said, "Tell your father that Esqueda is dead and don't belittle the part you had in it. Tell him Martin's dead. Tell him all of it."

"You still figurin' to run the settlement?" Antrim asked.

"Yes."

"He ain't goin' to like that none," Roan opined.

"Then tell him to learn to like it," Brazos said, wheeling his horse. He rode toward his own place.

The movers, he noticed, had taken up land, and shelter was going up. Fallers were in the timber three miles beyond and several ox teams were moving back and forth, snaking logs. Passing Ryker's settlement house, Brazos nodded to Ryker who stood in the doorway with Modry. He was halfway to his own place when Martha came to the doorway of his cabin and stood motionless while he covered the remaining distance and dismounted stiffly.

Emma came out, her eyes wrinkled against the sharp sunlight. She looked around for Martin and Brazos said, "He stayed over there, Emma."

"Stayed?" Her eyes were round and bewildered. She waited, wanting to hear words, but he found that he

191

could tell her no part of the truth.

Finally he said, "He loved you, Emma. That was what he said at the last."

He saw the measure of relief push aside her grief and she nodded. "I guess I knew that," she said, remembering the night he had left, that first tenderness he had shown toward her. She turned and walked toward the settlement. Brazos watched her, then pushed past Martha and went inside his store. She had the goods on the shelves and had been doing business. Three barrels of sauerkraut were stacked in the back room, along with sacked grain and some home-cured meats. She came in and went behind the counter. He supposed he should tell her that her brother was dead, but she already knew that.

"There won't be any more trouble," he said. "Esqueda's dead."

She shook her head in disagreement. "Maybe not the kind he brought, but there'll be trouble. I'd hate to live in this world without it." She removed the cloth from a round of horncheese. "I imagine you're hungry."

She cut him a thick slice and gave him some bread and sliced ham. He ate most of this, then said, "I found Antrim and Roan. There'll be no more trouble from Jeb either."

"He's not a man who'll listen good," she said. "Are you sure you can handle him?"

"I can handle him," Brazos said with finality and she did not question him further. He finished his meal and shoved the plate aside. "You remember once when you asked me what the wind said to me?" He glanced at her and smiled. "I guess I know now."

"I'm glad," Martha said, "because for a long time I thought I was the only one who heard it." She crossed her arms and studied him carefully. "You're older,

Brazos. And I think I like you better when you're your own man."

He sighed and looked around the store. "One of these days I'll make a sign and hang it out front. More fittin' for a man to show he's in business."

She came around the counter with a soft smile and touched him briefly. He smiled back and kissed her. "I've been waitin' for that," she said.

"The waitin's over," he said. "Course, there's a speck of work to be done around here yet. I ought to go to Fort Davis in the mornin' and bring back another train of supplies."

He glanced at her and caught her frown, then went out and to his cabin. He shaved carefully and scrubbed with soap. Martha had made him a new pair of breeches and he put on a store-bought wool shirt. In the afternoon he walked to the settlement and talked to Ryker. Men sought him out for opinions and he was not flustered by this attention, but answered them gravely. The sun was well down when he walked back to his own cabin. In the air the odor of fresh-turned earth was strong and from across the flats he heard the laughter of children. He stopped and listened to this sound. After he began to walk on he could still hear it and he knew that this land had changed.

A danger had been lifted and men moved with a new spirit of freedom. Tomorrow he would go back to Fort Davis and by traveling over the trail, convince other men that it could be done. Perhaps Captain Travers would be sufficiently impressed to send a message to the President to encourage migration. The speculation pleased him.

Martha had the evening meal ready and he sat down to eat.

"You through gaddin' for the day?" she asked. A

glance told him that she was not angry.

"Guess I am," he admitted.

"While you was at Ryker's, did you make any mention of marryin' me?"

He looked up from his plate. "Seems that I did."

She smiled and finished her meal. Afterward he went outside and sat on the step, listening to the new sounds. He could hear voices coming across the flats. Martha had lighted one of the new coal-oil lamps and the brightness shot through the doorway, casting a long shadow of him on the ground. He heard her stirring around inside and went in, taking a seat at the table.

Martha seemingly paid no attention to him as she removed the large wooden tub from the wall peg. She emptied two fire-buckets of water into it and raised a foot to take off her slippers. Padding barefoot across the floor, she took a cake of soap from the cupboard and dropped it into the water.

He said, "That water's for fire, you know."

"There won't be any fire tonight," she said and reached behind her to unbutton her dress. It came loose and she let it slide from her shoulders until they were bare. "Do you have to watch me?"

He studied her eyes; there, he had learned, was the clue to her moods. They regarded him with sharp slivers of mischief in them and he came over to her. Pushing the dress gently off her shoulders, he heard it whisper as it fell. He looked at her and there was no change in his expression except that his fingers bit more sharply into her bare shoulders. She said, "Are you goin' to Fort Davis in the mornin'?"

"I guess it can wait," he admitted. She smiled when he added, "You goin' to wash, then don't be all night about it."

We hope that you enjoyed reading this
Sagebrush Large Print Western.
If you would like to read more Sagebrush titles,
ask your librarian or contact the Publishers:

United States and Canada

Thomas T. Beeler, *Publisher*
Post Office Box 659
Hampton Falls, New Hampshire 03844-0659
(800) 818-7574

**United Kingdom, Eire, and
the Republic of South Africa**

Isis Publishing Ltd
7 Centremead
Osney Mead
Oxford OX2 0ES England
(01865) 250333

Australia and New Zealand

Bolinda Publishing Pty. Ltd.
17 Mohr Street
Tullamarine, 3043, Victoria, Australia
(016103) 9338 0666

MG ✓
9/02

ML